baboon king the

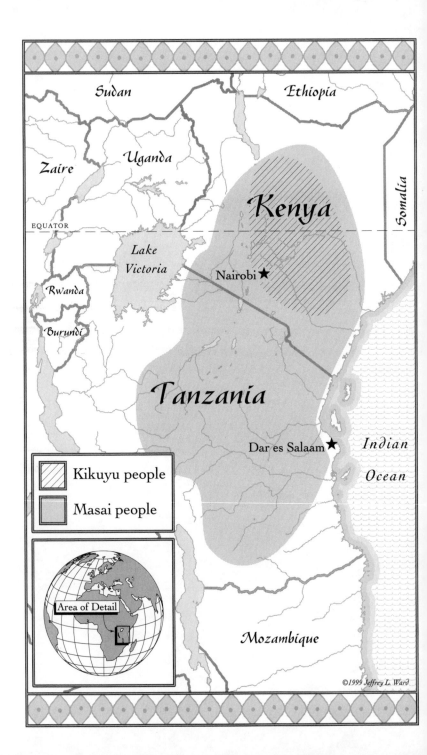

baboon king
the

anton quintana

translated by john nieuwenhuizen

Walker and Company   New York

Originally published in 1982 as *De havianenkoning* in the Netherlands.
First English language edition published in 1996 in Australia;
this edition published in the United States of America in 1999 by
Walker Publishing Company, Inc.

Library of Congress Cataloging-in-Publication Data
Quintana, Anton.
[Bavianenkoning. English.]
The baboon king/Anton Quintana; translated by John Nieuwenhuizen
p.   cm.
Summary: Son of a Kikuyu mother and a Masai herdsman father, Morengáru the hunter
lives on the edges of tribal society until an actual banishment forces him to make a life
for himself among a troop of baboons.
ISBN 0-8027-8711-8
[1. Baboons Fiction. 2. Kikuyu (African people)—Fiction. 3. Masai (African
people)—Fiction. 4. Africa Fiction.]
I. Nieuwenhuizen, John. II. Title.
PZ7.Q485Bag 1999   99-18322
[Fic]—dc21   CIP

Printed in the United States of America

2 4 6 8 10 9 7 5 3 1

PART I

the nature of the beast

1

The screams of the fringed monkeys in the treetops made it easy to track the leopard's progress. The noise accompanied him all the way. Jumping from branch to branch, the monkeys followed him right to the edge of the forest, and kept yelling abuse from the very last tree.

He hated those loudmouths, but he could never climb fast enough to grab one of them. He knew that, and so did they. But if one of the rowdy troublemakers ever got down too low . . .

The leopard was large for his kind: eight feet from his nose to the tip of his tail. His unusually pale fur stood out against the dark tree trunks, so he preferred the brownish yellow hills. Despite his size, he was shy and liked to stay in hiding during the day. But sometimes the heat on the open plain drove him to the cool forest. It was better there, as long as the monkeys didn't notice him.

The plain looked arid, yellow-brown, the color of everything in this landscape. Yet there was life in the grass stalks. With the first rains, the grass would shoot up tall and green again, topped with swaying white plumes. Then the temperature would drop, and for a time, the leopard would be free of the monkeys.

Once more he looked back, growled, then slipped away into the tall grass. He made himself as flat as possible, and began to run with his white belly almost against the ground.

3

The stiff stalks did not hinder him, as he used one of the many long tunnels the warthogs had made through the grass. These warthog tunnels went off in all directions, but the leopard knew where he was going and raced through the passages of crackling stalks. He didn't need to worry about meeting warthogs; in the dry season they moved to low-lying hollows, looking for mud baths, and that was just as well, because he had a healthy respect for their vicious tusks.

As soon as he reached the first hilltop, he stopped. This was his regular lookout. He lay down under a whistling thornbush. It was covered in gallnuts riddled with ant holes, and the wind whistled through them. He liked that sound.

The scene was familiar. On one side was the plain, covered in acacia, thornbushes, and tall grass. The red glow of the setting sun made it look as if it were on fire. For years he had hunted on that plain in the old way: waiting in a tree for prey to come by. He had caught impala and gnu, and also little procavia and mice. But for the last half year, his hunting grounds had been in the opposite direction. That was where the humans lived. They thought they could lock their cattle safely inside enclosures of thorny branches.

The terrain there was more difficult for hunting. The humans had cut down the forest, burned the thorn scrub, and churned up the soil. But some areas of no-man's land were left among the farms, stretches of rough ground where no fires glowed in the night. Still good hunting to be had there.

Since the leopard had killed a tame animal—accidentally, really, that first time—he had shifted his hunting ground. It didn't bother him that this was farther away, because he could be certain of his prey. Domesticated animals couldn't escape.

He started crossing the hills, while the red sun shrank

away at the end of the plain. His lithe body passed smoothly under low silver-leaved shrubs. Three more times he used a low hill for a lookout. At the last hill he had to make a detour to avoid a troop of baboons, but he had anticipated that; the tall mimosa farther along was their sleeping tree.

If they felt threatened, baboons wouldn't hesitate to attack a leopard. The adult males were fierce fighters. He took good care to stay out of sight. From a safe distance, he watched the troop go by: scouts in front, then the females and young, the males bringing up the rear.

Unnoticed, the leopard moved on, not stopping again until much farther along. He sniffed the air.

Small animals nearby dropped to the ground, motionless, waiting for him to disappear. He heard and saw nothing, didn't even pick up any scents, but he knew they were there. They didn't interest him. He was drawn by one scent, which was gradually getting stronger: the scent of humans.

Once, long ago, that scent had filled him with fear. Now, though no longer frightened, he was always watchful. He went on at an easy pace, avoiding any ray of light in the gathering darkness.

He reached a palisade of thorny branches. Again, he stood still and sniffed the air: the warm smell of cattle packed close together. He crept around the enclosure. The cows inside started moving restlessly. They had caught his scent. If he couldn't find an opening somewhere, he would jump over those prickly branches.

The smoke of smoldering charcoal warned him. Not far off, a small fire glowed like a watchful eye. He knew there had to be a hut, built close against the palisade. An easy way over. But there would also be a human.

The leopard lay down. He pressed his spotted body flat

against the ground, his head between his forepaws. He watched the red glow. And waited.

Perhaps that light would go out later. He had time. In the *boma*, the cattle calmed down again. The night wind carried his scent away from them, into the hills. No sound came from the hut.

Slowly, the fire died down until it was no more than a spark.

2

In the hut, the herdsmen were disturbed by the agitated movement of the cattle. Before they were properly awake they knew the reason: a leopard.

They grabbed their spears. They were *nyama*, spear-carriers of the Kikuyu tribe, and their task was to protect the cattle. They threw off the soft brown goatskin cloaks that hung from shoulder to knee. Naked, they ran outside.

The alarm was raised with high-pitched herdsmen's cries that cut through the night, rising above the bellowing of the frightened animals.

"Leopard!" they called. "Leopard!" And the *nyama* in the other huts took up the cry in the same shrill tones. "Leopard! Leopard!" Now everyone knew what was going on. They were all alert, armed, and ready for anything.

Torches flared, hissing and crackling, and a fierce, ghostly light dispelled the darkness. Through the billowing yellow-gray smoke the herdsmen stepped into the *boma*. They carried their long spears poised over their shoulders, ready to thrust with maximum force.

In a flash, the leopard came flying over the palisade, fastened his claws in the back of a calf, and bit through the bleating animal's throat. Then, growling, he stayed there gripping the twitching animal, as if he wanted to go on enjoying the effect of his deadly bite. Maddened with fear, the cows pushed and jostled each other against the furthest side of the enclosure.

The *nyama* came with their torches and spears to surround him. Slowly, unwillingly, the leopard moved back a little, letting his blood-covered mouth sink between his paws. He drew his hind legs up underneath his body, all his muscles taut for the leap to safety.

As one, the *nyama* ran at him, snarling like the leopard himself. Twenty paces away they stopped, bounced a few times on their right feet and hurled their spears.

The leopard moved so unexpectedly and so fast that most of the spears missed. One spear hit and stuck, quivering, in his rump, but it didn't hinder him. Instead of leaping away over the palisade, the leopard charged the *nyama*. With one swipe of his paw, he managed to wound four of the young men.

Overwhelmed by such fierceness, the herdsmen recoiled. Except one, who was as courageous as the great cat. He drew his razor-sharp *parang* and ran shouting at the animal. But before he could use the knife, the leopard was on top of him. The great incisors bit into one of his shoulders, while the long hind legs tore his lower body to pieces.

When the other herdsmen rushed to help their friend, the leopard let go of his victim, turned, and disappeared over the palisade in one fluid movement.

It took a while for the *nyama* to come to their senses. They lifted the injured man from the dung-covered ground and carried him to the nearest hut. They left a wide trail of blood.

For a long time, the cows shuffled about near the fence, their eyes large and mad-looking in the light of the torches. Even when they calmed down, not a single one dared go anywhere near the blood.

The injured *nyama*'s friends sat around him in despair, their faces wretched. By the flickering firelight, their wounds looked like unreal, gaping holes.

The dying man made no sound. A cold sweat glistened on his ashen face. No one tried to reassure him falsely. He knew that death was coming for him. Death would eat him, swallow him, digest him, and then it would be the hyenas' turn. He was not afraid, for there was nothing more to be afraid of. This was simply the end. But he was sad, because he had wanted to experience so much more. He was just eighteen.

He died before morning.

3

"This leopard has to die," said Mauro, the village headman. "He must be put out of action, and quickly, too. He has now learned how easy it is to kill a man. A human is no match for a leopard; he has no teeth, no claws, no hooves, nothing. From now on, this leopard will kill people."

Mauro ought to know what he was talking about. He had been alive at the time when the Kikuyu were still hunters. The young men listened to him in awe. Behind his bald head, they saw the sun rising—"proud as a spear-carrier." Its rays flashed like fiery spears over the hills, so that mimosas and acacias seemed to burst into flame. That was a heartening sight. The sun was an immortal *nyama*.

Somewhere in the hills, in a place only his mother and sisters were allowed to know, lay the dead *nyama*.

It was better that way. No one knew in what mortal form he would want to live on. The hyenas would free him from his dead husk. There, in the hills, he would have enough time and space to choose. Perhaps, one day, he would return to the village of his own free will. If that happened, the wise men would know. At the birth of a boy they would consult the entrails of a goat, which would reveal to them that the brave *nyama* had returned to his people.

"May I ask a question, wise *mundumugu*?"

The old man turned and nodded.

"Doesn't a man have his spear? Does the leopard not know that a man, too, can be dangerous?"

Mauro's beady eyes were all but hidden by the folds of his eyelids. He sat staring thoughtfully for a while, his chin resting on hands folded over the knob of his ceremonial staff. This was carved in the shape of a water-buffalo head. The wood had been polished smooth by many years of use, and now resembled old ivory. Mauro's venerable appearance matched the beautiful staff. You would never see him without that symbol of his rank, or without the many thin copper neckbands that made it hard for him to hold his wrinkly neck straight. To wear even two of those bands showed you were wealthy!

"That is very true, my boy," answered Mauro finally. "But that is exactly what makes this leopard more dangerous than ever. Just think of our women and children, who have to go far from the village to get water. Who have to cut firewood on the edge of the hills. They do not carry spears. From today, this leopard is going to know the difference between a human with a spear and a human without one."

He stretched his arm out toward the hills and said, "That is why I appeal to you! Don't wait! Don't give the leopard a chance to recover. Go and find him! Kill him! Go in large numbers and follow his trail! Drive him from his hiding place! Give him no rest! Kill the leopard who is after our women and children!"

"And after our cows," one of the *nyama* added.

"And after our cows," Mauro agreed. He glared suspiciously at the boy, but saw only trusting eyes, betraying no ulterior motive. Reassured, he nodded solemnly. "I have spoken. Go now, quickly, before the trail fades."

Satisfied, Mauro watched the young men, the proud spear-carriers of his village, descending the hill with agile leaps, their rust-brown cloaks flapping in the breeze and the metal tips of their spears glinting in the sun. For a long time he could hear their eager voices on the thin morning air. At the bottom of the hill they spread out and started searching all the shrubs and thickets. Soon one of them proudly held up a spike of grass. He had found blood. From there on they went faster; they knew in which direction to search.

As the sunlight strengthened, their spirits lifted. Last night's terror seemed forgotten. It wasn't long before Mauro could hear their singing rising from the undulating grass. Not just any song, but a fitting war song beginning with an outburst of raucous yells and ending on a long-held trill.

Mauro turned to the two boys who had stayed behind to

accompany him to the village. Casually, he asked whose calf had been killed. When he heard the name he nodded sympathetically, hiding the relief he felt. Not one of his own. As long as the *nyama* managed to find the wounded leopard quickly, he could stop worrying.

If he peered intently, squinting against the glaring light, he could just follow the *nyama*'s route through the tall grass. But soon the sunlight became too harsh. He sighed and turned away. What could a man do but wait? He just hoped they would be brave and persistent, those spear-carriers of his, and not give up too easily.

He would make an offering to the god Ngay today, asking him to help the *nyama*. They would need that support because, even if they managed to follow the track to the end, the leopard would be waiting, cornered. . . . But what was the point of worrying about that? It was the *nyama*'s task to protect the cattle, it always had been. It was a pity they no longer had experience with predators these days, but the job had to be done all the same. Even if things went wrong, he could not be held responsible.

The sun climbed higher, warming his chilled bones. The dew on the grass began to evaporate. In a moment he would start his own descent. He wanted to be back in his own yard before it became too hot. He might be able to sleep in the shade for an hour or so. The mere thought of it made Mauro's eyelids feel heavy.

When he couldn't see or hear them anymore, Mauro forgot about the spear-carriers. He bent his inscrutable face over a trembling cobweb on which dewdrops were still glittering. Beautiful. Why did a man have to grow old before he learned to enjoy things like that? Mauro couldn't help smiling.

The two *nyama*, whose thoughts were with the hunters, saw his smile and exchanged surprised looks. What was there to smile about? Was Mauro thinking about amusing things, while they could think only of the fate of their friends? How could the wise village headman grin at nothing, after all that had happened last night?

4

A Kikuyu was always surrounded by gardens and cultivated fields. One *shamba* bordering the next one, as far as the eye could see. A view of round huts, green hedges, twisting paths and fruit trees. It was quite common for a Kikuyu not to see a single wild animal for years, even though, just a few miles away, they roamed the plains by the thousands. You knew that herds of zebra and gnu moved along the Ngong hills every season, because you could see the enormous clouds of dust stirred up by all those hooves. But a right-minded Kikuyu wasn't the slightest bit curious about all that game.

Even in times of hunger—when the harvest failed through lack of rain, or because of too much rain at once, or when the locusts, those "teeth of the wind," had devoured everything that grew—even then, the Kikuyu were not interested in game. What use was it to you if the place was teeming with antelope and gazelle, when eating their meat was taboo? The only meat a Kikuyu was allowed to eat was that of domesticated animals: chickens, goats, cattle.

A *nyama* did not learn to hunt. From his childhood he was taught that hunting was barbaric. A man only hunted if he had no gardens and no cattle. But a true Kikuyu took care not to live such a primitive existence. It was shameful enough to know that his ancestors had depended on hunting, before they had learned about agriculture and cattle breeding.

So it wasn't all that strange that the *nyama* lost the leopard's track. They had never learned the finer points of tracking. Yet they didn't want to give up. Stubbornly, they kept searching in the heat of the open plain. But stubbornness wasn't enough.

There were too many obstacles. All those impenetrable stands of thornbushes to work around, only to discover that the tracks didn't go on. Was the leopard hiding in that thorny tangle? There was nothing for it but to hurl stones into the bushes, just to make sure he wasn't in there. And those stretches where the soil was so parched it seemed like dust. There, every footprint was visible—except when the wind blew away the top layer, tracks and all. Even worse were the limestone ridges, with no imprints whatever, so that, after hours of searching, you started imagining that every little scratch must have been made by the leopard's claws.

By midday, the sun scorched their shaved heads like a branding iron. Dust caked their sweating bodies. They had long since stopped singing. Grim and determined, they searched on. Once again the trail came to a dead end, this time in a gully full of thistles and spiderwebs, where adders slept on stones heated by the sun, and scorpions guarded the countless cracks. Dispirited, the *nyama* squatted down. They could barely look each other in the eye.

Quietly, they began to discuss what was to be done. They would never find the leopard, that was clear. It would be better to return to the *boma*, but all they would be able to do there was wait. Was there any other solution?

"Morengáru!"

One of them called out the name as if it was the answer. And, of course, it was.

Of course. Morengáru! The Kikuyu with the heart of a hunter!

Morengáru lived by hunting. He bartered skins for corn, milk, and yams. He traded antelope meat with passing Somalis, in exchange for copper ornaments. It was rumored that he even ate game himself. In the eyes of the other Kikuyu, Morengáru was a barbarian, content with a simple hunter's life, and too stupid to be a farmer.

But now . . .

"If Morengáru can't do it, no one can."

"We must go and talk to him."

"Talk to Morengáru? The elders will have to do that."

5

In time-honored Kikuyu tradition, elaborate meetings would have to be held, for who was going to pay Morengáru, the hunter, for his services? And would the other villages in the Ngong be prepared to take part?

It seemed that the leopard had recovered quickly from his wound, because he returned twice before the village heads could come together for a meeting. Each time, he killed a calf. Each time, he was too fast for the *nyama*. Once he even managed to jump over the palisade carrying a newborn calf and disappear with it.

Finally, the Kikuyu leaders gathered on the highest hill in the Ngong, where the *boma* was. They sat in a circle and were offered milk and corn cakes. Thuo, being the eldest, opened the meeting.

"We are agreed that it is this same leopard who robs all our *bomas*. Something urgently needs to be done about this scourge. It has been suggested that we involve Morengáru. Who agrees with this?"

The other wise men pondered Thuo's words, gazing expressionlessly into the blue distance over the hills. Finally, one said, "It is not fitting for a Kikuyu to hunt, as this Morengáru appears to do. Should we now reward his misconduct by entrusting him with this honored task? What does the head of his village think about it?"

Mauro looked sullen. "I have always advised Morengáru against hunting," he replied. "Should I now encourage him in this kind of behavior?"

"We have no choice," said his neighbor. "The leopard has to be killed."

"Can the *nyama* not do that?"

"They have lost the trail again and again," replied Thuo. "I, too, regret the necessity of involving someone like Morengáru, but, on the other hand, too much damage has already been done. The safety of our *nyama* is also at stake. Therefore, I propose that we call on this Morengáru."

When no one voiced further objections, Thuo called one of the *nyama*. The boy approached timidly. Never before had he seen so many wise men together.

"Fetch Morengáru," was the order.

And the *nyama* hoisted his cloak up over his shoulders, so

he could run freely, and hurried, loose-limbed, down the hills toward the village.

6

Morengáru's *shamba* was a disgrace. His hut, of palm fronds and reeds, with a pointed roof of woven papyrus, looked neglected. He had no sheds and stables. He didn't even have a vegetable garden.

A proper *shamba* was an oasis in the dry hill country. You would see corn growing higher than your head and hear millet rustling in the wind. When you entered the yard of stamped earth, you would fall over children, chickens, goats. Wood pigeons would be cooing in the cedars, the only forest trees left, spared to provide shade.

But in Morengáru's yard, instead of the sweet scent of overripe pumpkins, all you could smell was the sharp odor of urine, which he kept in earthenware jars to use for tanning hides. Not a tree, not even a hedge. Dust swirled, because the wind had free play. How could anyone live like that? It was easy to see that Morengáru had been brought up by nomads.

Thuo's messenger found Morengáru in front of his hut, scraping the skin of a kudu and covering it with salt. For a moment, the *nyama* stood watching, openmouthed. His bald head gleamed in the midday sun. Flies swarmed around his eyes, big blue-green horseflies among them. He killed a few, until he caught Morengáru's mocking glance. Immediately,

16

the *nyama* adopted the stance of the spear-carrier. He put his spear—symbol of his new dignity—straight up beside him and tried to look as if nothing could upset him. So he stood, immobile, while the horseflies crawled over his eyelids and the dust swirled around him. Fortunately, Morengáru seemed to know how a *nyama* should be welcomed. Even if this particular *nyama* had only just passed through his initiation. His hair had not even begun to grow again. Without a word, Morengáru produced a hollow gourd of corn beer, which he handed to the boy.

The *nyama* did not thank him. As a spear-carrier, he was entitled to this welcome. He drank the appropriate amount—and an extra gulp because Morengáru wasn't watching anyway—and said, "Thuo calls for you."

Morengáru went back to his work as if he had never been interrupted. The boy looked at him incredulously, then repeated his message more loudly. If a village elder wanted to speak to you, you dropped everything and came instantly.

"Thuo wants to speak to me?" asked Morengáru. "What about?"

The cheek! He would find out when he squatted down before Thuo. The *nyama* said nothing. His look was sufficient answer.

Morengáru's face reminded him uncomfortably of the Masai. He was paler, and his lips were a bit too thick, but otherwise he had that thin, slightly curved nose, those widely spaced, narrow eyes. And that haughty look. Only a Masai could look like that.

But Morengáru was no Masai, even if he had Masai blood. He was a Kikuyu, and should observe Kikuyu customs.

"You must have run pretty fast," said Morengáru. "Have another drink."

17

The *nyama* shook off his irritation and drank greedily, holding the gourd high above his mouth. He could feel the alcohol going to his head. He had only been allowed to drink beer since his initiation as a *nyama*, so he hadn't had much experience. A bit frightened, he lowered the gourd.

Morengáru grinned, not nastily this time, but as if he could remember exactly how his first beer had tasted. The boy grinned back, a bit hazily.

"This is strong *pombe*," he praised like an expert, returning the gourd with an appreciative clack of his tongue.

Morengáru took one gulp to clear his mouth of dust and flies, then let the beer pour gurgling straight into his throat. The boy, still thirsty, couldn't help mimicking the action, his Adam's apple moving up and down in time with Morengáru's. Morengáru choked with laughter.

Shamed, the *nyama* turned away. To cover his embarrassment, he pointed his spear at the highest hill and said in a commanding tone, "Thuo waits."

Morengáru nodded slowly. "What does Thuo want with me?"

"You'll hear when you get there," the boy replied, trying to look as challenging as he dared.

Morengáru looked like a real Masai again as he laughed. "Do you expect me to walk with you all that way without knowing what for?"

The *nyama* didn't reply.

"And what if there's something I should have brought?" Morengáru asked cunningly. "Something I need, to do what Thuo wants from me. Then I'd have to come all the way back to get it, and keep Thuo waiting. . . ."

The *nyama* tried to think, but his head was heavy from the beer. Sighing, he gave in. "It's about the leopard," he said.

"You're joking," Morengáru laughed.

The *nyama* looked at him with undisguised hatred. "Are we going?" he asked.

"We're going," replied Morengáru cheerfully.

7

"You walk ahead," said Morengáru, when he emerged from his hut. He was now wearing a monkey-skin cape over his shoulders, with a short parang tied under his right armpit. He carried a long spear, with a metal blade at least twenty inches long. His bow hung from a loop sewed onto his brown cape.

The boy gaped, not at the fearsome spear—a real *moran* spear!—but at the quiver of arrows. Their tips were carefully wrapped in dried grass.

"Are they poisonous?" he asked.

Morengáru shrugged. "A bit."

The *nyama* couldn't take his eyes off the arrows. "Do you make the poison yourself?"

Morengáru didn't reply. Everyone had his own secrets. No need to tell the boy about the white sap of the candelabra plant, a single drop of which was enough to make you go blind. Or about the wabai root, more poisonous than the black mamba. "I thought we were in a hurry," he said.

The young Kikuyu jogged along beside him, still curious.

Morengáru marveled at how fast things changed. Here was this corn-eater getting all excited about something as simple as arrow poison. Yet his great-grandfather had been a hunter!

"How fast does it work?" the boy wanted to know.

Morengáru stopped, in the middle of a path between two gardens.

"How fast? What does that matter? How certain, that's what you need to know. If you're hit with this, you're as good as dead. All I have to do is walk behind you until you fall over. And now, my brave *nyama*, you can walk ahead of me. All you have to do is show me the way to the meeting place."

Offended, the boy started running down the winding path, clutching his spear under his arm. Morengáru followed him with a mischievous grin. Soon, they left the last of the *shambas* behind. The path became little more than a faint track leading up and down the hills. There was no one to be seen, except the lonely young goatherds. They watched Morengáru with their dark, moist eyes, waving their small wooden spears. One day, they too would become real *nyama*.

Crickets made a strident, monotonous noise everywhere. Their rhythm became part of the throbbing of the hot air and the trembling of the tall grass. Everything vibrated. Nearby hills, distant hills, everything. The shrilling of millions of insects reverberated like the shimmering of the sun itself. Light and sound became one. That was the voice of heat, penetrating and soporific, inescapable.

Morengáru had never seen Thuo, who must be the most important of the Kikuyu leaders, but he wasn't really curious about him. His thoughts were focused on Mauro. Mauro would be sitting comfortably in the shade, amply supplied with fresh milk. Morengáru didn't envy him this privilege. He knew only too well why he was answering Thuo's call. It was worth his while to be walking in the heat of the day. His day for relaxing in the shade would come.

Now there were more and more thornbushes to detour around. The grass was hard and brown. Termite hills rose above it, the wind whistling around their polished tops. The *nyama*'s supple body had disappeared in the sea of grass plumes. But Morengáru calmly kept his own pace. Occasionally he could just see the boy's head bobbing up and down on the waves of yellow-brown grass. The Kikuyu did his best to stay ahead. He wouldn't allow himself time to catch his breath with this half-Masai behind him.

Morengáru stopped in the shade of some acacias. He leaned against a smooth trunk, grinning. He was really only pausing to allow the boy to keep his lead.

Those farmers' sons were so weak and untrained. They thought they were real warriors if they were allowed to hold a spear. It was different in the past. Then, Kikuyu were impressive warriors, but now they liked their comfort too well. Their *shambas* produced plenty. They didn't need to go on raids.

If Kikuyu boys still felt the need for adventure, there was, fortunately, the *boma* in the hills. There, they could guard the cattle and camp in the wilderness. The *nyama* imagined they had been through a baptism of fire merely because they returned to the village unscathed. Then they would be spoiled by the whole family, and the unmarried girls of the village would dance for them. After four years at the *boma* they could stay down in the village, get married, and start their own farm. And then spend the rest of their lives reminiscing with the other veterans.

Compare that with the training of a Masai. . . . They left their parents when they turned twelve, and were only allowed back when they were thirty. All those years they wandered through the wilderness with the herds.

Morengáru walked on, his mind back with the Masai, until he stopped the stream of memories, because he was becoming

21

depressed. Instead, he thought of the village elders who were waiting for him up there. Especially Mauro, the most powerful man in his village. His grandfather, on his mother's side. When he thought of Mauro, he couldn't help smirking. He had a surprise in store for that old tyrant.

The heat pressed like a weight on his shoulders. He realized now he had drunk too much beer. Imagine how that *nyama* must be feeling. Suddenly he noticed the metal of a spear glinting in the grass. There was the boy, resting in the shade of a thornbush. Silently he looked at Morengáru, clearly ashamed at his weakness, but still with a challenge in his eyes. At first Morengáru wanted to keep walking, but then he changed his mind. He squatted, putting his quiver full of arrows down in front of him.

"Do you need a lot of that poison?" asked the boy.

"Enough to cover the tip of a knife," said Morengáru. "Then you've had it. Then all you want is to go to sleep."

"To sleep?"

"Yes. To sleep." Morengáru looked around, as if he was afraid the leopard was listening. His face close to the boy's, he continued softly, "Just a scratch, and the poison starts working. It creeps through your blood. And then you become sleepy. Not just a bit sleepy, no, more sleepy than you've ever been in your life. All you want is to lie down. You just *have* to sleep. You're so tired all of a sudden, you want to be dead. Even if your pursuers are right behind you. Even if you could be caught any moment. You just couldn't care less any more. As long as you can go to sleep . . ."

The boy's eyes grew large. His mouth slowly sagged open. He looked scared and foolish, hypnotized by Morengáru's low voice and sinister look. Until, suddenly, Morengáru laughed loudly. That broke the spell. The *nyama* jumped up.

He wanted to say something, but couldn't speak. So he just stood there, shaking with fury. Morengáru stopped laughing. If he didn't watch it, the boy would attack him. And that wasn't really what he'd had in mind.

When the *nyama* saw that Morengáru was doing his best not to laugh, he calmed down. Without a word, he turned round and hurled himself at the wall of grass. Morengáru shook his head and decided to wait a little. But his wicked sense of fun was too strong for him, and he set off after the *nyama*. He ran through the grass like a wild savanna dog, with the easy stride he could keep up for hours, and soon caught up with the tired Kikuyu. Morengáru slipped past, laughing at him as he went. Then he ran on, not looking back, with a smile of contempt for that amazed, sweaty face. Occasionally he leaped high, so he could look over the top of the grass for a moment. Even when he was way out of the *nyama*'s reach, he kept running. Not because he was in a hurry, or because he didn't want to keep the village heads waiting, but simply because it was the easiest way for him to move.

8

As Morengáru squatted amongst the *nyama*, he could smell their typical body odor: the slightly sweet scent of plant eaters. The odor of the Masai was very different, much stronger and more rank. They're grazers, he thought, once again wondering why he stayed with these people. But he admitted straight away that he had little choice, so he adopted his usual haughty stance.

The grass had been full of *jigga*, and a few of them had gotten under his toenails. He had to pick them out with a thorn immediately, before they could lay their eggs and cause nasty ulcers. While he was busy doing that, he saw how curiously the *nyama* were looking at his equipment. But they asked no questions. They were *nyama* after all, men of few words.

At the bottom of the hill, the village heads sat in their meeting. Mauro stood up and beckoned him with his staff. Unhurriedly, Morengáru descended the hill. When he came to the circle of old men, he planted his spear firmly in the ground and stood waiting, proud and tall.

Mauro addressed him somewhat absently, almost indifferently, making it clear that, as far as he was concerned, this conversation was unnecessary; he spoke only because the others had insisted.

Had Morengáru heard about the leopard?

Which leopard?

Which leopard did he think?

Very quickly, Mauro's voice acquired a sharp edge. Morengáru's pretense of ignorance annoyed him. His piercing, beady eyes searched for signs of spite, but his grandson knew how to keep a straight face.

Mauro liked to put on a show of fatherly concern. If he punished young people who ignored his lectures, it was only because he was worried about them. It was not ill will, but wisdom. He intended the best for them. It saddened him that he had to correct the young so often. But he knew his responsibility. Who else would remind the Kikuyu of their obligations to the elders? Youth owed it to the Council of the Wise to pay attention and obey.

And if it so happened that he disliked Morengáru, he

wouldn't let it make any difference. Mauro was above such things, at least that's what he wanted everyone to believe.

But Morengáru knew better. That's why he had looked forward to this as he climbed the hills.

"Of course I can catch the leopard for you. Give me two cows, that's all I ask."

"Two cows!"

"I won't do it for less."

For the Kikuyu, owning cattle was a sign of wealth. Apart from his fields and gardens, an ordinary person might perhaps own a few goats and chickens. But cows meant capital. Twenty goats would normally buy a wife. How many wives you could buy for a cow was an open question. In practice, the question never arose, seeing as a man was not allowed to have more than three wives anyway. Only someone who had farmed successfully for many years could even start thinking about a cow. And now this Morengáru had the gall to ask for no less than two cows.

While the elders conferred, he stood waiting, cool and collected, leaning on his spear, one leg pulled up like a stork. He knew that the leopard could cost them more cows in the long run. They begrudged him his reward, but they had no choice.

Mauro was the one who got most worked up. It was blackmail! Scandalous! Any *nyama* would consider the task an honor!

Thuo clacked his tongue disapprovingly, but for the rest kept quiet. The debate would go on for quite a while, even though the outcome was known already. All this served only to allow Mauro to save face. After all, it was Mauro who would have to watch the impudent Masai showing off the cows he had earned so easily.

Mauro became more and more indignant. They should all know why he would vote against. Morengáru was no good. He set no store by the old established Kikuyu traditions. He chose to live by hunting. And now that single, barbarous talent would make him rich. They shouldn't allow themselves to be coerced by this half-Masai.

Mauro calling Morengáru a half-Masai in his fury caused secret amusement amongst the old men. Not that anything showed on their inscrutable faces, but they turned away to spit in the grass. And as they did so, they exchanged eloquent glances. Their eyes gleamed in the sunlight.

Mauro, of all people, needn't remind them that Morengáru was half Masai! As if they could forget for a moment. As if they didn't all know how this had come to be so. Mauro had really struck a wrong note there. Perhaps he realized it himself, for he kept quiet from then on. He glared around the circle, looking for a gleam of mockery, of gloating. But the others, too, were old hands at this game and were very careful not to let their thoughts show.

Only Thuo looked as if he was laughing, but that was because of his peculiar teeth. A lifetime ago, Thuo had his eyeteeth knocked out and replaced with artfully carved ivory fangs, like a predator's. These days, no one would think of doing anything like that. After all, they weren't savages, like the Masai, who loved showing off in lion skins.

Meanwhile, a decision had to be made. The Council of the Wise began to realize that the discussion had reached an impasse. Not that there was anything wrong with that, as long as the discussion was well conducted and dignified.

9

His Masai father may not have left him anything, but Morengáru had certainly inherited his malicious sense of humor. He was having a great time. But it must be said in his favor: He could laugh just as hard at himself.

Here he stood, half Masai, half Kikuyu. He was not at home anywhere, nor welcome with anyone. Yet soon two cows, large as life, would be his. What a fantastic joke!

Droughts, locusts, and floods would always keep the ordinary Kikuyu down. And if that didn't, the village heads would, by driving up the cost of essential ceremonies. You could not do anything—get married, become a father, start cultivating a new field, bury someone—without a sacrifice of two or three goats. That was called tradition. The Council of the Wise adhered to that fanatically. As long as ordinary people had to work constantly, they had neither time nor energy to worry about community affairs, so the elders did that for them. And you could only become part of their council if you were a man of substance. So the Wise Ones stayed in control.

With the Masai, it was enough if you proved your courage. Then you counted. The Wanderobo automatically selected the best hunter as their leader. With the Somali you had to be of good family. But with the Kikuyu, wealth was the shortest way to power.

And a person's wealth began with cows. Who knew how many cows Morengáru would eventually own if he started off today with a cow and a bull! Wasn't Mauro himself the living example of the prosperity such a pair could bring? Had he not started out exactly like that twenty years ago?

Would Mauro be aware of what lay behind the high price Morengáru was asking?

As far as Morengáru was concerned, the old men could go on deliberating for hours. Ridiculous, the way they sat there whispering, their heads together, like conspirators. Morengáru turned his face away and laughed into the wind, his eyes half shut against the dust. But he was not aware how provocative he appeared. He didn't notice how the old men looked up at him with the unanimity of a flock of vultures.

Once more, without hope of success, the patriarch of the Ngong tried to persuade Morengáru that he should adopt a more modest approach. That it was his duty to kill the leopard, rather than a service only to the rich of the village.

"The leopard actually only eats beef," Morengáru replied laconically. "So it's only fair that the owners of the beef cattle pay me."

"But, young man," Thuo countered in a friendly voice, lisping a bit through his artificial teeth, "the leopard is also a threat to the lives of the *nyama*. Doesn't that argument strike you?"

Morengáru realized to his surprise that he didn't mind this Thuo. He would almost bet that this most senior elder was secretly enjoying the situation. The way he sat there watching, with those clever eyes. Perhaps Thuo was beginning to see what was really going on. So Morengáru replied with a great show of respect. That would make all the more clear how little respect he had for Mauro.

"Wise great-grandfather of the Kikuyu. For years, no *nyama* has been injured, unless he hit his own foot with his knife. For too long the spear-carriers have been able to sleep around their fire. Now the leopard has come to give them a chance to prove they are brave *nyama*. They should really welcome the leopard."

Thuo turned his wrinkled face away from Morengáru and

spat forcefully over his shoulder. Then he looked at the young man, long and intently.

"Am I mistaken," he asked, "or do I hear the Masai in Morengáru speaking now? Tell me, brave heart, is it still the custom among the Masai for every boy to kill a lion before he can call himself a *moran*?"

"That is still the custom," Morengáru replied. He knew what question should follow, but, strangely enough, it was not asked.

Why, the others wondered, did Thuo pass up this chance to belittle Morengáru? How easy it would have been to ask this boaster if he had killed a lion himself. By what right did he dare talk about the courage of the *nyama*? But Thuo obviously didn't think it necessary to put Morengáru in his place. And the others didn't dare interrupt him.

Morengáru noticed how critically the old men were looking at him. They were obviously wondering why he had no scars, not even a scratch, to show that he had ever faced the teeth and claws of a lion. They must have concluded that, when it came to it, he had the tame heart of the Kikuyu. That was obviously the reason he had returned to his mother's people. He could feel their appraising looks on his naked, unmarked body.

Involuntarily he recalled the hideous scars he had seen among the Masai. Scars from injuries that completely deformed a body, that had cost eyes, that had totally paralyzed muscles. But always scars a *moran* liked showing in public. Signs of honor.

Silently, Morengáru let the condescending looks of the Council of the Wise pass over him. He raised his upper lip in a furtive little laugh, full of self-mockery, because he had to submit to the judgment of these corn-eaters.

Thuo smiled indulgently. He began rolling one of his long earlobes between thumb and index finger. He exchanged a glance with Mauro, who obviously didn't think there was anything to smile about. It was already late in the afternoon. The grass was waving restlessly in the rising wind. From the direction of the village came young boys carrying baskets of glowing charcoal. Soon the watch fires would flame up in the dark. If a decision wasn't made soon, another night would be lost. And perhaps another calf.

"All right then, Morengáru, kill the leopard for us and we'll give you two cows."

"A cow and a bull."

"That is understood."

"Healthy and fully grown, but not too old."

"As you say."

"And they have to be the same color."

"The same color? Why is that?"

"Because that's the way it has to be. They both have to be black and white."

Thuo looked questioningly over his shoulder at Mauro, who nodded, grim-faced.

Had Mauro finally got the message? A bull and a cow the same color! Black and white! Or had he forgotten what color his own first cows had been?

10

The calf stood in a cage built of thin sticks bound together, outside the *boma*. From where he was sitting, Morengáru could only just discern the animal. But this was the darkest hour of the night. Soon the moon would rise, and he would be able to see down the hill as far as the acacias in the valley. He expected the leopard from that direction.

This was his fifth night. Straight after sunset he had crawled into the pit with its covering of branches. He had dug the pit just below the brow of the hill so that the branches did not stick out over the hilltop. He could look out through a slit. When the time came, all he would have to do was to stand up, push the branches away, and draw his bow. From a distance, his shelter looked just like a shrub.

As always, night had come quickly. In the brief twilight, you could hear the cawing of the long-beaked crows and, in the distance, the farewell cry of an eagle. An invisible ostrich signed off by drumming loudly. Then all became silent. The sun rolled away behind a mountaintop like a glowing coal falling through a grate, leaving nothing but black ashes. Night.

Morengáru was hoping that the leopard wouldn't choose this hour for his visit. While it was so dark, the nose and eyes of the calf were all he could rely on. The calf was now used to being apart from the herd, and while it was quietly ruminating, you could assume the leopard was not nearby.

He had worked out his position very carefully. The leopard would want to use the cover of the last acacias before crossing to the *boma*. And, on his way, he would find the lonely calf. Of course he could not get at the animal because of the strong cage, but he would have to discover that for

31

himself. And by that time, another discovery would be waiting for him.

As was his habit, Morengáru waited motionlessly. Once crouched in an ambush, he made no unnecessary movement until the moment for action came. All he did was look and listen; listen intently to the sounds of the night.

Out there, there were always animals wandering about who had every reason to be on their guard. They signaled to each other—the arrival of a predator, for instance—and all who were tuned in could understand the meaning of their signals. But for the moment, no alarms could be heard. The stars came out one by one, followed by the moon. The clear light sharply outlined every shape, making the deep shadows all the more mysterious.

Two, three hours passed. Then a silence fell, so intense that it was like an alarm in itself. Not even a cricket could be heard. Morengáru looked at the calf. It was standing stock-still in the middle of its cage. Suddenly the high whine of a jackal cut through the silence, immediately answered by a scream from another hill. Morengáru took a deep breath. The watchers in the night had faithfully carried out their duty. He knew the leopard was on its way.

Slowly the whining died away. The leopard must have passed the jackals' hunting grounds. No matter how hard Morengáru peered, he could not make out anything among the acacias. Half an hour passed, then an hour. Strange. The leopard should have been here long ago.

A sensation of danger gripped Morengáru. He had often been warned like this by his hunter's instinct. Experience had taught him not to reason but to immediately obey this instinct. The leopard must have somehow discovered his presence, and was now stalking *him*. Was perhaps at this very moment ready to spring . . . ?

Courage wasn't enough in a moment like this. It was not courage that made you do the right thing, but coolheadedness, even if you broke into a cold sweat all over.

If the leopard was not on the slope in front of him, nor in the shadows of the acacias, there was only one other possibility. It must have somehow got behind him. Slowly, Morengáru turned round in his narrow pit and peered out through the branches. But nothing stirred on that side of the slope. He should now feel reassured, and yet . . .

Morengáru leaned his bow against the side of the pit. He took up his spear. If the leopard was as close as his instinct told him, arrows would be useless.

Again he carefully scanned all his surroundings. Where could the beast be hiding? He saw nothing, yet he was certain it was very close.

Then two things happened simultaneously. The calf started to bleat, staring intently in Morengáru's direction, and inside the pit, a dead leaf fluttered down from the cover of branches. It landed with a soft warning tap on Morengáru's shoulder.

It had to be: The leopard was on the roof of the shelter. No wonder Morengáru couldn't see him anywhere!

There was not a second to be lost. He knew he had no chance of crawling out in one piece. On hands and knees he would be in a helpless position. But he could not stay in the pit, either.

He thrust his spear upward through the branches. A frenzy of noise erupted above him. Savage claws ripped the branches apart, letting in moonlight and the gaping mouth of the leopard.

33

There was no room for an upward sweep with the *parang*. Morengáru was stuck tight, caught in his own trap, half buried under splintering branches and the weight of the raging leopard. For one brief moment he looked straight into those crazed eyes, then they were gone. In his leap, the leopard dragged the last of the branches with him.

There stood Morengáru, head and shoulders out of the pit, totally unprotected. He watched the leopard disappearing with long bounds toward the acacias.

Slowly Morengáru climbed out and sat on the grass to recover. His mind blank, he stared toward the trees, while the wind dried the sweat on his body. Then he pulled his spear from his ruined hideout. In the moonlight, the blood on the metal blade looked black.

Good. The leopard would leave a trail of blood across the hills. All he had to do was wait for daylight.

The calf was still staring at him with wild eyes, but it was no longer shaking. Morengáru stretched himself out full length on the grass. He allowed the cold wind to gradually chill his body. He lay motionless, staring up at the stars. The cold, penetrating right down to his bones, was welcome. Unmistakable proof that, although he shouldn't be, he was still alive.

11

When Morengáru started following the leopard's trail, he felt miserable with cold. And that wouldn't get better for a while, as the sun was only barely above the hills. The tall grass and the shrubs were covered with dew, so he became soaking wet. But he didn't want to lose any time. Later on he would get warm enough! He found blood, and not just a little, under the acacias, so the trail was easy to follow. Occasionally he came to a spot where the leopard had rested. There, the grass was bright red. He cursed the wind that carried his scent ahead of him and would chase the leopard on for as long as he could walk.

The trail went up and down the hills. Gradually the traces of blood became fewer and fainter. They began to turn black in the sun. In the end it became so difficult to follow the trail that he had to keep looking to the last spot of blood he had found, as far back as sixty feet, while searching for the next one. The heat must have dried the wound.

The sun climbed higher, and it was as if its rays were reflected back by the red earth. Morengáru kept searching doggedly, very slowly now. Over slopes covered in stones and through hollows full of dust, and up again through the thorn-bushes. Somewhere in a gully, he lost the trail completely. He walked round in an ever-widening circle and carried on searching. It took two hours before he found a blood spot again.

The heat was becoming unbearable. Occasionally he stopped to pluck a long blade of grass and use it to skim the sweat off his forehead. In the afternoon he lost the trail again, but then he could see the edge of the forest in the distance. It was obvious that the leopard was hiding there.

Tracking was really nothing but being able to put yourself in the place of the animal you were pursuing. Below the first cedars, he found proof that he was right: new blood traces. From that moment on, Morengáru moved forward very carefully, ready for anything. He wouldn't be the first hunter who became so absorbed in the tracking that he forgot the prey itself, so that the roles could be unexpectedly reversed! He did his best not to make a sound, and kept his bow drawn.

Crouched low, he followed the trail through the tree trunks and thought about the leopard as he had seen him that night by moonlight. The fury of the beast had made a deep impression on him. Even now he felt awe, though he knew that the raider of the Ngong was doomed.

He reached a spot where the leopard had recently been lying under the bushes. The grass had not yet had time to stand up again. From there, the trail led up to a dense thicket of wild olives. It would be impossible to follow the trail through that tangle of branches. No matter how carefully he moved, he would make a noise. And after having been pursued all morning, it was just as likely that the leopard, in his hideout, would decide that enough was enough. In that case, he would have the advantage of surprise. He could easily keep dead still until the hunter had passed him, and then attack from behind.

Morengáru had just decided to make a detour, to finish up above the olive trees, when he heard the warning cry of a fringed monkey. He froze and peered upward until he discovered the sentry in the treetops. The monkey kept repeating its warning. The *nyama* could learn from these monkeys. If one was keeping watch, he wouldn't let anything distract him. These animals knew that the safety of the whole troop depended on each individual. All the females and young had hidden at the first cry.

From the direction in which the sentry was looking, Morengáru deduced that he was not the cause of the alarm.

It had to be the leopard. He could turn this to his advantage. By watching the sentry, he could work out where the leopard was hiding. So he waited. The monkey kept screeching and looking down toward a particular bush.

Morengáru sprinted, bent low, through the tree trunks toward the bush. This caused even greater panic in the agitated sentry, who saw himself suddenly confronted by *two* attackers. He could not know, of course, who was really under attack. As soon as Morengáru stopped, he looked up at the screaming monkey. It looked first at Morengáru, then to a spot to his left, and back again. He was now keeping an eye on both the human and the great cat. Morengáru raced on. Stopped again. Looked up. Now the sentry kept staring in Morengáru's direction. That could only mean one thing: Both intruders were in his field of vision. The leopard must be really close.

Morengáru peered intently into the shadows. Bit by bit he looked higher up through the shadows cast by the top branches. And there, hidden behind trembling leaves, the leopard had made itself as small as it could.

Fast as lightning, Morengáru raised his bow, drawing back the string in the same movement. But the leopard was just as fast. It landed like a snarling fury at Morengáru's feet. . . .

12

The leopard had had enough. Even here, in his shelter on the other side of the hills, this human dared pursue him. In his rage, the leopard hardly felt the arrow hit him. He tried to hurl himself at the human, who darted behind the thick, knobbly tree trunks.

The leopard slowed in his attack. He growled. The human waited for him, motionless. Again the leopard went on the attack, and again he lost his speed. He lowered his heavy head and coughed. The human seemed to be fading. The screeching of the monkeys came to him as if from far away.

In his confusion, the leopard forgot the human who had provoked him so intensely. He slumped. In a daze, he looked at his forepaws, trying to stay upright. Then he started crawling backward, growling, afraid of something invisible that he imagined in front of him. He clawed slowly at the blades of grass, which rebounded, one by one.

He wanted to sleep. Just sleep. Vaguely, he was aware that he was not safe where he lay, unshielded in the grass. He tried to keep his eyes open, but soon gave up the effort. Perhaps the human was still there, perhaps not. He no longer cared. As long as he could sleep.

PART 2

the heart of the hunter

13

So now Morengáru was the owner of a bull and a cow. Big, healthy animals, and—as he had demanded—both the same color. Everybody was talking about it enviously. When Morengáru wasn't out in the hills hunting, he came up to the *boma* to inspect his animals. And to have a chat with Kiribai and Bajabi, two *nyama* with whom he had become quite friendly. They recognized him as an ally; they, too, were secretly opposed to the Council's power.

They had good reason to be. They were the sons of hardworking farmers, and both would, within six months, be allowed to settle down and start their own farms. And each had lost his heart to a lovely *bibi*, who had regularly come to dance for him. If you could believe their stories, the girls had shown their love in other ways, too. Kiribai and Bajabi really wanted to get married. But among the Kikuyu, getting married wasn't a simple matter. Listening to them complain, Morengáru barely managed to hide his amusement. Here was another example of the elders' tactics. No bargain was struck, no agreement reached, no ceremony performed, without them being involved. And so it was in this case. Who else would benefit from the bride price being constantly pushed up?

A boy contemplating marriage was forced into debt. No prospective father-in-law concerned about his reputation

41

could afford to ask too little for his daughter. The old men had made sure of this. And so a recently married *nyama* had to keep his nose clean while being up to his ears in debt. By the time he was old enough to voice his opinions, he would usually have a daughter of his own to marry off. No wonder things hadn't changed much.

No wonder, either, that Kiribai and Bajabi thought hard before asking permission to marry their *bibis*. But meanwhile another problem had been added to their woes. Recently, Mauro's first wife had died. The funeral ceremonies had made a great impression on the village. But it was clear to everyone that Mauro wasn't going to be content for long with just two wives. The law allowed him three wives. And the village head knew better than anyone what was due to a man of his standing. Soon, there were whispers that Ngatia, the most beautiful of the young village women, had caught his eye. Bajabi's beloved. It wouldn't be the first time that a rich old man had snatched a girl from her admirer.

And why not, Morengáru reflected. The rich were in control, and everything revolved around property. Mauro was one of the few who could pay cash for his bride. And wouldn't every father want such a powerful man for a son-in-law? That the groom was seventy didn't really come into it. Even the bride must surely see that being in love is a passing phase, while comfort lasts a lifetime. Only the rejected lover might look at it differently.

As soon as he was alone with his friends, Bajabi would complain bitterly—but softly. That's what amused Morengáru more than anything.

"What would you do in my place?" Bajabi demanded.

"Me?" asked Morengáru dreamily. Instead of answering,

he spat in the grass. There, on the slope, his two cows grazed among the others. He was content. All the same, he couldn't pass up the chance to stir the *nyama*'s feelings against Mauro.

"You know," he said finally, "I would promise her father everything he asked."

"But he's asking so much!"

"Even so, you should agree. Then marry Ngatia, take good care to make her happy, and give her a son as soon as possible. And by the time Father-in-law comes and demands his share, you start up a never-ending story. But you don't pay. Ever."

"But you can't do that," said Bajabi, shocked.

"Course you can. Just look at Mauro. Follow his example. Six months ago, he was supposed to have paid the potter. The poor wretch doesn't even dare ask for payment. Did you know he slaughtered his only goat because Mauro told him a sacrifice was needed? 'There is a *thahu* on your farm,' said Mauro. 'But, wise *mundumugu*, I only have one single goat, and my children need the milk.' 'Yes, that's a great shame, Ketabi. But you know the rules.' And so this idiot came and asked me to slaughter his one and only goat. Now he has no milk, and his children's bellies are swollen with hunger. And what do you think Mauro said when our good potter, after six months, went and asked for payment for the three large jars he had made? The wise *mundumugu* said, 'But, Ketabi, what is this all about? Didn't I advise you when there was a *thahu* on your house? Do you think that comes for free? We don't owe each other anything, my dear man. By the way, I'm very pleased with your jars. You can make me another three.'"

Morengáru rolled on his back laughing, his eyes squeezed shut against the sunlight. The two *nyama* felt uneasy at such lack of respect.

"Listen, Morengáru, it's easy for you to laugh. But if there's a *thahu* on your house, all you can do is make a sacrifice. That's how it's always been. That's not something Mauro has thought up."

"All the same. You should have seen the potter's face. And what's more, he walked for a day and a half to the river to find the clay for those jars!"

And Morengáru laughed once more. The young men looked at him uncertainly.

"What would you do, Morengáru, if you heard there was a *thahu* on your house?"

Careful, Morengáru thought. Careful with these two. They may have a lot of objections to the present state of affairs, but they're nowhere near ready for any real resistance. All those expensive *thahu*-complications are an important part of their existence. The Kikuyu need such complicated beliefs to give more meaning to their boring lives. But he couldn't really say things like that. Or that it required a certain courage to take a gamble on the unknown. A Kikuyu tried to provide himself with security at all cost, with protection against anything that could threaten him. Safety for the coming night, and preferably for the rest of his life. No wonder the *mundumugu* were so prosperous. Along with property, fear had entered the Kikuyu's lives. No other people had invented so many evil spirits. Not even the Wanderobo, who lived deep in the jungle, and so had every reason to be superstitious. But when it came to courage, the Wanderobo were still the descendants of the fearless Masai.

Morengáru realized the *nyama* were still waiting for his answer. He wasn't going to get out of it with a joke this time. So he said with a straight face, "Listen, you know I

44

don't have any goats. But of course I could try using the blood of a gazelle. . . ."

They stared at him incredulously. "But, Morengáru, you know such a sacrifice is useless. Just going out to hunt would bring down a new *thahu* on you."

"And here I was thinking it was *eating* game that was forbidden, not *hunting*," said Morengáru, feigning surprise. "And when the leopard appeared, hunting was suddenly all right. But, of course, that was a dangerous situation for the cattle. The evil spirits understand these things."

He stared past the boys, no longer seeing the cows, or even the hillside. His thoughts were somewhere else altogether, and they were clearly not cheerful. At last he seemed to come back to reality. "I'll tell you something," he said. "If Mauro had quietly accepted the leopard killing one calf after the other . . . or if he had waited until you *nyama* finally caught it . . . if he hadn't sent me after that leopard . . . I might have had respect for the old prophet of doom."

"The business with the leopard was an exception," said Kiribai. "It was a good thing you killed it. No one is going to hold it against you."

"Thank heavens for that," Morengáru laughed. "I was getting worried."

"But, seriously, you can't undo a *thahu* with the blood of a gazelle. So what would you do?"

"Immediately offer another sacrifice."

"But you don't have any goats."

"So I sacrifice another gazelle. And another and another and another, until the gods get used to them again. After all, they accepted them for centuries before we started keeping goats."

Kiribai and Bajabi stared at him, stunned. But they were

young, and here, high up on the hill, Mauro and his dire predictions seemed far away. Kiribai started laughing first, soon joined by Bajabi. The two *nyama* threw back their heads and laughed exuberantly in the sunlight. For want of something better to throw, they ripped up handfuls of grass and hurled it at Morengáru, shouting, "You barbarian! You savage!"

Morengáru joined in their laughter.

Long shouts reached them from the other hilltops, where there were also herdsmen. They meant: We can hear you're having a good time. What's it all about? Let us share the joke.

And Morengáru thought grimly: One day!

They would all have to realize that Mauro was just a smart talker. And once they could laugh at Mauro, his power would be finished.

14

As a young girl, Morengáru's mother had been sold to a passing Masai herdsman by her father, Mauro. The same Mauro who was now the village headman. That bargain had given the Kikuyu their first cows. At least, that's how the story went.

As Morengáru looked down the hill at his two cows, he thought they could just as well be those first cows. That first pair must have wandered there, grazing, just like his animals were now. And Mauro must have sat admiring them just as he was now. He hoped the old man would often take the trouble to climb up to the *boma*. Every time he saw Morengáru's two spotted cows, he would be reminded of how he himself had started out. And of the way he had acquired his first pair. It would make him think of an event he would rather forget.

To remind Mauro of what he had done twenty years ago had been Morengáru's only goal as he walked the long distance from his Masai home in the Loita hills to the Ngong. That was the reason he had come to live with the Kikuyu.

The old man must have realized this instantly when his forgotten grandson turned up. He would have been reminded of his youngest daughter—the one he'd married off to a Masai.

To a Masai! A nomad! A barbarian! Despite all his raving and ranting against mixing with other peoples over the years.

"It's not for nothing we Kikuyu have learned to provide for all our needs. So why get mixed up with Somali traders? Those no-good troublemakers. And why take up with Swahili scum who have had a bad influence on too many tribes already? Let every Kikuyu keep well away from that riffraff!"

Mauro preached against any form of contact with other tribes—against friendship with Kamba and Wanderobo, with Galla, Turkana, and Boran. But especially against mixing with the Masai. For the Masai were the archenemy, the pillagers from the past.

"They're drinkers of blood. They live in dung huts. They're unnatural parents who send their sons out to fight lions so they get murdered and maimed. An inferior race, who have made irrational bravery into a cult. If it were up to the Masai, the world would remain a wilderness forever. Who would want to have anything to do with the Masai?"

That's how Mauro had talked all his life, and still did. But it hadn't stopped him bartering his own daughter to a Masai.

To a herdsman who happened to be passing through and had offered a bull and a cow for the pretty Kikuyu girl, at a time when no Kikuyu could even begin to think of ever owning cattle. Mauro hadn't passed up his opportunity. And he justified an act so against his principles by the future benefits that flowed to the community.

This was how a father could allow his daughter to be carried off by an uncivilized cowherd, away from the green fields of the Ngong forever. A cowherd who would treat her as the lowest of his concubines once the harsh nomadic existence had destroyed her youth and beauty. A cowherd who would give her a son who would be held in contempt by everyone: a Kikuyu with Masai blood, or a Masai who was half Kikuyu. To think that such a creature could even exist!

15

No wonder Morengáru had finally left the hills of Loita and sought refuge in the Ngong—that idyllic place his mother had spoken about so often. But he had only left once his life with the Masai had become impossible.

The boys of his own age, with whom he spent all his days and nights, considered him inferior. They reminded him of it constantly. Not deliberately, to offend him, but out of sheer carelessness. It made no difference how often he proved that he was at least as strong and clever as they. He was still just a Kikuyu, and would never become a proper Masai.

Courage they respected, so he had been braver than any of them, but respect was not sympathy. He could not make friends, and remained an outsider. In the end he couldn't stand their superior attitude anymore. He decided to leave rather than suffer their contempt for another day.

He took off through the gorge that separated Masai country from the lands of the Kikuyu. Alone, with nothing but his bow and spear. He camped at the bottom of a gorge with walls so steep and regular you could look through it as far as your eye could reach. And he had gone on.

Through the winding mountain pass known as the Devil's Gate. Past an extinct volcano with caves so deep he didn't dare look into them. He had walked over black shiny shards of volcanic glass. Through white clouds of steam. Over ground that rumbled under his feet. But he had gone on.

Over slopes where the wind carried down clouds of steam, making you breathe in fire and sulfur, and over plains full of crevices where you could hear fierce bubblings. And through a swamp full of caustic water and stinking black mud covered in pink foam. But he had gone on.

Despite the mud that soaked the flesh off his bones. Despite the sodium crystals that scoured his feet till they were raw. He had trekked through the shimmering heat of gravel fields, where the water in every puddle was bitter. Ever farther.

Until he had seen the Ngong hills in the blue distance.

And so he had arrived in the land of the Kikuyu, like a Masai who had walked through those hills as if they were his own. He wore his copper-colored cape and carried his long *moran* spear. His hair was tied in small knots and shone with fat. To the farmers looking up from their cornfields, he seemed an apparition; a ghost from the time when the Masai were still all-powerful and all the land and cattle belonged to them. But Morengáru was unaware of this. He walked into

49

his mother's village as a traveler who has finally reached his destination.

And so he appeared in front of Mauro's hut. The moment Morengáru started talking—in the high tones of the Masai, but speaking the language of the Kikuyu—the old man realized who was standing before him. He listened, his face closed. And the whole village had listened in. It was curious to hear their own language spoken in the strange manner of the Masai—a cross between speaking and singing.

Mauro's grandson. The son of you-know-who, who had, long ago, you-know-what . . .

Instantly, everyone remembered. It became a brand-new event. Mauro's twenty-year-old deed shocked the village all over again. There stood the living proof of Mauro's betrayal of his own principles. A Kikuyu-Masai.

Whatever Mauro thought privately, he could not refuse Morengáru entry into the village. The boy had every right to live with his mother's people if that was what he requested. And that was exactly what Morengáru did. He sought shelter with the Kikuyu, explaining nothing.

He stayed, and realized that his mother's glowing tales had been memories colored by nostalgia. The Ngong was not the lost paradise. He was too much a child of nomads to be moved by the rhythm of sowing and harvesting. He couldn't understand how a man could become attached to a piece of land, just because he had put years of work into it. He could be looking at a field, seeing nothing but a mass of green growth, when an ancient, wrinkled Kikuyu woman would turn up, chop a hole in the tangle of tough stems, and produce an enormous yam. That sort of thing was a mystery to a herdsman.

Apparently, to a Kikuyu, there was no more beautiful sight

than a plot of cultivated land. Their culture was totally foreign to Morengáru, and he settled in very slowly. Farming was not what he wanted to do, so he decided to make a living by hunting. He ignored the criticism this provoked. His neighbors' disgust with his bloody trade only amused him. And he couldn't possibly take all that Mauro said seriously.

16

Kiribai and Bajabi had come to help him build a hut. In exchange, they expected corn beer and tall tales about the Masai. Beer they got, but no stories.

Solid and good-humored, those two. Real Kikuyu. Proudly they showed him how a proper hut was built. He had been used to the low, dome-shaped huts of the Masai, built from a mix of mud and dung, dried rock-hard by the sun. But Kiribai and Bajabi cut tough saplings for the frame and brought their sisters to weave reed matting for the walls and roof. The hut had to be put up in a single day. A half-completed hut could be invaded during the night by an evil spirit that would be impossible to drive away. For the same reason the hut had to be round; spirits could easily hide in corners. Strange that Morengáru didn't know such things.

"And don't ever leave things lying around outside; that attracts *fisi*."

It seemed the Kikuyu feared nothing as much as a visit from *fisi*, the hyena. After all, you could never know who was visiting you—whose spirit had entered *fisi* while his body was being devoured.

After more beer, the *nyama* acted out a pantomime of the despised animal. They mimicked its skulking walk, its hind-quarters dragging low, its head shaking foolishly. They imitated the way *fisi* will slink off when disturbed, with a high-pitched whine, looking back with stupid eyes. They enjoyed themselves enormously, trying to outdo each other. But Morengáru was reminded of children laughing away their fear. All the same, it was bad luck to discover one morning that *fisi* had defecated in your yard. That would cost you at least two goats: one for a sacrifice and one to pay the *mundumugu*.

So goats were brought inside every evening. And very cozy that was, too. Kikuyu liked the smoky darkness of a locked-up hut, chock-full of belching goats chewing the cud. They liked their clean breath and sweet smell, particularly in the morning, when, still half asleep, your cheek against their fur, you started to milk them. Nothing was as delicious as the taste of fresh, warm milk. And it was lovely to go to sleep with the familiar scrabbling of the goats underneath the bed you'd built high up above the floor.

Yet a Kikuyu wouldn't brag about his cattle, the way a Masai would. A Masai would get carried away once he began talking about his cows. How fat and healthy and fertile they were, how much milk they gave and how much blood he could take from them daily without weakening them. A Masai would sing the praises of his property, his voice rising above the plain with the smoke of his fire. His herd was his glory. A man who didn't boast about his cattle wasn't considered a proper man. But Kikuyu preferred to act poor, so as not to give thieves ideas. And perhaps they were right. After all, they were not famous as fighters, like the Masai.

Finally Morengáru learned from Kiribai and Bajabi how

you always had to keep a fire burning in the center of your new hut. Smoke drove away lice. They also tried to guide him through the customs and traditions of the tribe. It wouldn't be their fault if Morengáru didn't fit in. He just had to adapt. Not think too much about his mother, who had languished in a crude hut made of dung. Not think too much about his own bitter youth spent among the drinkers of blood.

17

The corn harvest was safely in. That was a good reason for a *ngoma*, a great dance festival.

Anyone who had kept an emergency store of corncobs could now use that to brew beer. For days, beer stood fermenting in every hut, gently bubbling and foaming. In the wealthier *shambas* a kid was fattened on the leaves of sweet potato plants. Festive hats and copper ornaments were polished, cloaks and aprons brushed, and the great drum appeared. From time to time a drum roll was heard, then it was silent again. It took much patience and expertise to warm up such a big drum, and the drummer took his time over it. He was aware that every unexpected roll sent shivers of excitement through the whole village.

So great was the excitement that no one could bear to stay in their own *shamba*. Many visits were made, and there were a lot more fires than on ordinary evenings. People were already singing. On the day of the *ngoma*, you could see the participants coming from a long way off, but you could hear them from even farther. The music of wooden flutes and small drums was heard from every path.

Everyone went to the open area just outside the village where the dance would be held. More and more groups headed there, all bringing food and drink. Some visitors had walked twenty miles. The *nyama*, in particular, were richly dressed, resplendent in waving ostrich feathers and long monkey tails and carrying wooden rattles. The *bibis* were shiny with oil and draped with every bit of copper wire they could lay their hands on.

The real dancers wore no ornaments at all but had smeared their naked bodies from top to toe with a pale red chalk, making them exotic, almost like a separate race of people. They led the dancing, and you could hear their cries clearly above the music.

A *ngoma* by day was always genial and exuberant. Visitors from other villages sat in groups around the dance area, talking and nibbling sweets, happy to see each other again. Children ran around wildly, imitating the dancers. All the young people took part in the dancing, tireless as long as the drums sounded. They stamped, jumped, twisted, and shouted with abandon. And all around this colorful movement lay the unchangeable hill country of the Ngong—a vista so wide that this whole crowd of people was lost the moment you glanced away.

Morengáru wanted to disappear into those hills for as long as the *ngoma* lasted. He had not brought in any harvest, so he had nothing to celebrate. No matter how hard Bajabi and Kiribai insisted that he join in, he refused. It seemed as if he felt above something as simple as singing and dancing. Haughtily he strode away, and the Kikuyu watched him go, shaking their heads.

Why did Morengáru have to make such an exhibition of himself? Why couldn't he ever just join in?

18

When people in the village were really cheerful, Morengáru always wondered if they were laughing at him. That was why he preferred to keep to himself. He didn't dare trust anyone. There were a few people in the village with whom he felt a bond, but they were outsiders too. Loners, like him, who went their own way. He had to admit the Kikuyu didn't mind if you were different. They let outsiders live in peace.

He had more or less become friends with three men, each of them happily eccentric, who took as little notice of their neighbors as he did.

Kariuki, for instance, quietly neglected his vegetable garden because he preferred making music. The others couldn't understand it, but of course it was his own business. When his garden produced practically nothing, they laughed at him openly. But no one tried to change Kariuki. If Kariuki wanted to stay a poor musician, that was his affair.

And Kupanya. He didn't have a garden at all, except for a tiny herb garden. He had proclaimed himself an herb doctor and went about with his bag full of plants and his head full of prescriptions. He brewed medicines for all sorts of ills— eye diseases, skin afflictions, intestinal disorders; he had something for every kind of illness. Yet he didn't have a great future as a medicine man, for he always prescribed herbs you could simply pick in the wild. If anything made Kikuyu laugh, it was a ridiculous lack of business sense. Besides, Kupanya couldn't stand the sight of blood, so he avoided messing around with the innards of goats and chickens. His medicines would work perfectly well without all that, he always said. He just couldn't get it into his head that a right-thinking Kikuyu would feel cheated without a bit of magic.

It had taken Morengáru a while to get used to Kupanya, for though he was a man, his character was really feminine. He could take you by surprise at times with a really girlish gesture or laugh. At first, Morengáru had been surprised to hear Kupanya shamelessly burst into giggles or see him walk away wriggling his bottom like a *bibi*. He found it hard to believe he didn't do it deliberately. But after a time he took no notice of such things. This same Kupanya, who squealed if something frightened him, went off by himself looking for herbs in the wilderness and waited calmly for a family of lions to go by. How many of those *nyama*, who demonstrated their masculinity by laughing at Kupanya, could match that? But nobody forced Kupanya to behave like the other men. Nobody made him become a *nyama*. Anyway, Kupanya would look ridiculous with a spear.

And then there was Kimani. His neighbors understood Kimani even less. By day, Kimani seemed an ordinary farmer, just like them, working hard in his field. But the Kimani who settled himself comfortably in his yard in the evening, with a gourd of corn beer between his knees, was a different Kimani altogether. He talked nonstop. And anyone who cared was welcome to listen to his crazy stories. He made them up on the spot without ever laughing himself. Kimani spent his evenings alone, because not many Kikuyu felt at ease with him. Yet even without an audience Kimani talked ceaselessly, his rough voice loud in the dark, occasionally rising, and then suddenly breaking off because he had reached the punch line of his story. There was a sad silence when there was no one to laugh at the end of each story, but soon enough Kimani launched enthusiastically into the next one. If he ever noticed the silence himself, he would shout a hearty greeting at the pale face of the moon.

Morengáru could listen to Kimani for hours. He talked about remote places as if he had been there himself, and had some amazing stories. About countries where it rained constantly—or never. About valleys filled with the cold white dust that covered the top of Kilimanjaro—dust that melted into nothing in your hand. Of course Kimani was a bit mad, but his stories had a logic of their own.

Kariuki, Kupanya, and Kimani had slowly changed the way Morengáru saw the Kikuyu community. They showed him the possibility of being different, something that would never have been accepted by the Masai.

Poor Kupanya, who couldn't stand the sight of blood. His life would have been impossible in the Loita hills. How could he ever have won his *moran* spear? And yet this same Kupanya wandered through hills that teemed with wild animals. Wasn't that courage?

Why should there be only one kind of courage? Why only *moran* courage? Was the superior attitude of the Masai partly a lack of insight?

At that thought, Morengáru felt guilty but, strangely enough, also relieved. He was still troubled by the fact that the Masai hadn't been prepared to accept him as an equal. Why wouldn't they, if courage was what made a man? What difference did it make then if you were half Kikuyu?

So, bit by bit, Morengáru began to doubt. Thoughts arose

that he had learned to suppress long ago, when he realized that he was the only one with such doubts.

He remembered the *morans* who traveled from one Masai village to the next to show the little boys their horrific scars. They were welcome celebrities, who came to tell the young about the glorious fight with their first lion. They traveled around for years, because if they missed a village people felt cheated. What he remembered best was the way these mutilated men told their stories. It could have been the thousandth time they told a story, but it was still alive with their amazement and delight. Their whole existence revolved around that single moment of truth. But didn't all the years before and since mean anything? Did a Masai ever wonder if one single hour of glory was worth having to live as an invalid for years and years? Such questions simply didn't occur to them. And anyone who did wonder about such things was obviously not made of the right stuff.

19

A famous *mundumugu* arrived at the *ngoma*. Surrounded by *nyama*, he strode into the dance area, but not to dance. Yet there was still a lot of energy left in that old body. With a spring in his step he walked past the rows of spectators, half singing, half declaiming, one hand covering his mouth as if he was telling a secret. His speech went on for a long time, but his listeners didn't get bored. They soon became a chorus, repeating the last words of every sentence, ever louder and more wildly. Morengáru, on the other side of the hill, could follow the speech as if he were right there.

The same old story. The laws of the tribe. Prosperity. Magnificent future. The Kikuyu deserved to own all the land.

Morengáru got fed up with that gleeful singsong voice and wandered farther into the hills, even more gloomy than before.

Finally he sat down under a large mimosa tree. Here not even the sound of the drums reached him. The branches above his head were covered in prickles, but the trunk was smooth enough to lean against. And so Morengáru sat dozing in the heat of the afternoon.

And, like the spirit of a restless ancestor visiting in your sleep, a silent, insubstantial shadow approached the slumbering Morengáru. So intense was the afternoon light that the shadow was visible through his tightly closed eyelids. The sudden blocking of that light was enough to make the hunter Morengáru wake instantly. Ready for anything, absolutely still, he opened his eyes a little.

He saw a tall shape, black against the blue sky. Without opening his eyes farther, he couldn't see much more than two forelegs. Black knee joints and shiny black hooves. Beyond that, sandy-colored skin. That was enough to recognize the animal he had to deal with: an oryx. Amazed, he wondered how this could be. There was no animal on the savanna as shy as this antelope.

As he cautiously raised his eyes he could see the black lines beside the eyes, and then the large, quivering ears. The shoulders had deep scars from many fights. And then Morengáru saw the horn.

No antelope had more beautiful horns than the oryx. Long, slender, ringed, curved-back horns—prized hunting trophies but also dangerous weapons. A cornered oryx could stab right through you with their deadly points.

This oryx had only one horn. The other one had been broken off just above the head, in a fight no doubt. But that single horn was superb. Morengáru had never seen such a beautiful specimen before. At least three feet long, and as sharp as a dagger.

The old bull was probably a loner, expelled from the herd for his aggressiveness, condemned to the lonely, meaningless existence of an exile.

Had this recluse approached out of curiosity, just to inspect the sleeping human? Now that Morengáru had opened his eyes fully, the great antelope slowly drew away. From the way he danced back, on his graceful but solid legs, you could tell how strong and heavy he must be. He was watchful, but not afraid. The way he lowered his head, his single horn pointed, quivering, at Morengáru's chest, the old bull even began to take on a challenging air.

Seconds passed. Morengáru sat motionless, too enthralled to be afraid. In the large, dark eyes of the oryx he could see his reflection: a tiny squatting man with ludicrously large hands and knees. The distortion in the convex mirrors made him appear to have a bent little body growing out of the tree trunk behind him.

Morengáru's mind was a blank. He kept looking at his own face in those moist pupils, then he pulled his lips back in a grin. And in the oryx-eyes the miniature Morengáru smiled back at himself. Then the oryx blinked and the black mirrors disappeared for an instant. When they reappeared, those long lashes had wiped out reality. Morengáru's mirror-image had changed into that of a gaping baboon.

How was this possible? An optical illusion? A distorted reflection? But laughing at it didn't help—the mirror image laughed back, with the wide open snout of a baboon. This was no longer a distortion of reality. This was a different reality, and he didn't want anything to do with it. He wanted that animal to disappear.

Morengáru heard himself scream wildly. Startled, the oryx raised his head, and instantly his eyes, filled with sunlight, were just the panicky eyes of a terrified animal rearing backward, snorting. Clods of earth flew around Morengáru's ears. The oryx stormed away over the plain, twisting and turning as if trying to shake off a pursuer. When he finally disappeared behind the hills, Morengáru could hear the drumming of his hooves for a long time.

That's when Morengáru decided to get drunk. He went straight home and pulled the stopper out of the large gourd of corn beer. From the distance, the sounds of the *ngoma* reached him—high-pitched flutes and the rhythmic banging of two-toned drums—but it seemed to him that above everything he could still hear the drumming of the fleeing oryx's hooves.

20

Anyone familiar with life on the highlands knows the feeling of loss that overcomes people each evening when it grows dark. The immensely wide daytime world, which you can gaze over as far as your eyes will reach, suddenly becomes small.

All day long, nothing in the landscape stands higher than you and nothing gets in the way of your roving glance. You can look over the flat crowns of the few trees. Or else you can look through them. The innumerable tiny leaves filter the sunlight, but never form a solid screen. With all that space, you don't think about things that are unclear or doubtful. You live literally with your head in the sky. You can see the hazy clouds sailing by just above and feel the wind coming from infinitely far away. You can observe everything at once. The antelopes in the plain below, the weaver birds in the bushes nearby, you take them all in with one glance. Sometimes it becomes almost too much. Then the very sky seems to come to life. The heat causes mirages that reflect the landscape, and outstretched hills appear to stream toward the sun on glittering waves. At such moments the world becomes so grandiose and breathtaking, so incomprehensible and clear at the same time, that you can't think of anything insubstantial.

But when the light goes from the sky, everything changes. Knowing that the moon and the stars will soon light the world doesn't help. The clear sunlight is gone, and the world, once so wide, contracts to the size of your own yard. There you sit by the glow of your little fire. And faithfully waiting for you will be the doubts and questions that seemed so unreal by day. That's how it is every evening when dusk has driven you home.

After all the excitement of that long day, the Kikuyu had returned to their *shambas*, dead tired. No more flute music, no more small drums, no more jingling of bells, no more rattles. It seemed as if the festive spirit had gone with the light. Here and there a child could be heard crying, but otherwise everything was silent. Every sound seemed smothered by the falling darkness.

Morengáru squatted by the little fire in his yard, listening. He drank regularly from the large gourd of foaming beer and stared wide-eyed into the night. He had been with the Kikuyu long enough to know what would follow. He had been at harvest festivals before. When the sound finally came—the very start of the sound he had been waiting for—he growled softly, deep in his throat. The hair stood up on the back of his neck.

It began as a soft, plaintive moaning that was heart-breaking to hear. After the merriment of the day, this muted singing was like a fire slowly dying out. As if everyone was exhausted. And sad. As if the harvest festival was already over. Then, for the first time that day, the great drum could be heard, very softly. It was just a monotonous, slow throbbing; so indistinct you could almost ignore it, like a spark in the grass waiting for the wind. Faces appeared in doorways. Everyone seemed tired and weary, but that little spark still glowed. The soft throbbing made them aware of this tiny flame.

The drum sounded its first roll; encouraging, stimulating. Of course the festival couldn't be over yet, it was only beginning. Hesitantly, people started to come outside. Their shadows drifted in the glow of the many small fires. For a few moments the tired revelers moved uncertainly in that world without moon or stars. But the drummer knew how to speak to them through his accelerating rhythms, and soon they obeyed. Now the great drum beat louder, faster, insistently, with ever more strength and authority. Who could ignore its call?

Out of the darkness, Kikuyu came from all directions to the large meeting place among the *shambas*, carrying torches, so that it seemed the only lighted spot on earth. Now everyone was more serious and dignified than in the daytime. Men and women had dressed in long gowns, making them look regal. And that was how they felt, too. Gradually the stars became visible. For a long time there was no dancing at all, just singing. The many voices sounded like one in the night; harmonious, full of melancholy, sonorous and sincere.

Morengáru listened from his yard, poking listlessly at his fire. Dancing and singing like the Kikuyu was not for him.

For the Masai, dancing was a form of fighting. No young man would ever go to a dance feast without taking his spear. Like almost everything in their lives, dancing was a competitive trial of strength. The dancers would form a large circle and jump up and down, their heads thrown back. The trick was to stand perfectly still, then leap as high as possible, legs perfectly straight, arms tight by your sides. Five-foot leaps were quite common. But the important thing was control: A good dancer would often appear to hang still in the air for moments. For the Masai, a dance feast was nothing but a fight to the finish.

With the Kikuyu, dancing was something quite different. The men would make a long line, a centipede that then wound around the dance area, wriggling and stomping. Every dancer twisted, stamped, and moved to jingle his ornaments and rattles, but in doing so each dancer made allowance for the next one and tried to stay in step. So much togetherness didn't suit Morengáru.

The singing from the meeting place became louder and more enthusiastic. Morengáru listened, full of resentment as always. What do these peasants have to sing about? Not about fighting, obviously. But about their tame and monotonous little lives. Time to open another gourd. The Kikuyu sing about their corn and millet, about how pleased they are that the harvest is safely in. About how hard work is rewarded by abundance. That's what they sing about. Serious and melodious—celebrating their full stomachs, Morengáru thought. They have no other concerns or pride. And that drum, that great drum, so laboriously warmed up and tuned, is really the sound of their communal well-filled stomach.

It was an hour before the singing faded away. Then all Morengáru could hear was the drum. He kept drinking, and gradually it seemed that the drum began to question him. Provocative questions, to which he had no answers. What was he doing there all by himself? And why didn't he join in the festival? And who did he think he was? The drum asked such questions. Incessantly. Without waiting for an answer. All those pointless questions. What could be changed? That's what his life was like. There was no hope of change, unless some *mundumugu* turned up with real magic powers to make him a real Masai or a real Kikuyu.

The drum told Morengáru what was going on in his heart. The great drum, voice of the African continent, can do that. It may sound monotonous, but just as the beat of your heart can be fast or slow, glad or sad, so can the African drum. With its beat, now calm, now violent, it calls forth everything from your heart and drives you to the deepest thoughts. The beating of that great drum can leave you exhausted in the deep of the night, with nothing more to say. And you know that at the next feast it will again tell you what you don't want to hear.

Morengáru didn't want to wait for that moment. He knew the drum would defeat him sooner or later. He didn't want to hear that he was lonely. So he put the half-empty gourd under his arm and staggered in the direction of the brightly lit meeting place. There, the dancing had finally begun. In the flickering glow of torches, men and women lined up opposite each other. Their faces showed that they were totally engrossed in the rhythm of the drum. Their bodies shook with every beat. The drummer increased the tempo, and the movements became wilder. Louder and fiercer thumped the drum, and the dancers stamped in time, one heavy step forward, one backward. Their lithe bodies gleamed in the fireglow. The *bibis* waved colorful ribbons, making them stream around their arms and legs as they twisted and jumped. The dance area had been marked out by small fires, their glow barely reaching the spectators. Inside that bright circle, all the color and movement of the dancers came fantastically to life. Outside, it was as if the night had built a tall black wall—until the moon rose.

As the Kikuyu say jokingly: If we do our best, the moon will, too. What a moon! Large and transparent, it climbed above the hills, spreading a clear white light. In that pale glow, everything lost its own color, and the dancers became mysterious, as if they were no longer ordinary mortals, but shades or spirits. Anyone watching this spectacle had to feel that something as old as humankind itself was happening here.

Morengáru discovered that his second gourd was empty too. For a moment he stood, rocking back and forth, not knowing what to do. The people near him, who'd realized how drunk he was, nudged each other, grinning. What exactly he did next, Morengáru didn't really know. Perhaps the rhythm of the drum finally got hold of him. Perhaps he wanted to show how a real man should dance. Anyway, he soon became aware of loud laughter around him. He saw a line of bald crones at the edge of the dance area, slapping their thin thighs with delight, their toothless mouths wide open. Like crocodiles, he thought. What were these old wives yelling about? he wondered vaguely as he stood reeling and swaying.

He suddenly realized he was standing in the middle of the dance area and that all the laughter was about him, Morengáru. His leg muscles trembled. Red earth was stuck to his hands and elbows. And then he understood. He had tried to dance and, of course, had fallen over. Shame flamed through him, worse than any pain. Never had he felt so humiliated. And the worst of it was that he had brought it upon himself. He had come to the dance of his own free will, only to make a drunken laughingstock of himself in front of all these Kikuyu. If only he could dissolve, disappear. His legs lost all their strength. It was like walking on water. And the laughter behind him went on. The Kikuyu hadn't had such fun for ages.

21

The Kikuyu forgot Morengáru soon enough. The dancing and singing were much more important. As soon as he stumbled out of the circle, the lines closed up again. And Morengáru's idiotic behavior would have had no further consequences, if only . . .

One of the *nyama* didn't rejoin the dancers. He sat glaring after Morengáru for a long time, shaking his shaven head, laughing derisively. Just look at him now. Was this the same man who had so triumphantly overtaken him, Thuo's messenger, on the way to the *boma*?

Seeing Morengáru so vulnerable, lurching unsteadily, did him good. That'll take him down a peg or two, he said to himself. And while the others returned to the dance, the *nyama* nudged his best friend, signaling him to come away.

His friend looked surprised. He wanted to stay and dance. Though he let himself be dragged away, his arms and legs kept moving to the rhythm of the drum. He didn't understand what his friend wanted from him, and got no answer to his question. Once outside the glow of light from the *ngoma*, the *nyama* peered into the darkness to see where Morengáru had gone. When he saw him disappearing in the direction of his *shamba*, he nodded, pleased.

His friend went with him reluctantly. But when he realized they were following that staggering shape and understood they had to be quiet, he began to see what it was all about. He grinned and nodded in agreement. Of course he was going to be in it.

Silent as shadows, those two trailed Morengáru between the huts. They saw how he leaned on the low walls, and how once he stumbled and fell. They heard him cursing while he picked himself up. They shook their heads at each other, bursting with laughter. They were far from sober themselves, and couldn't think too clearly, but they were determined to teach that half-Masai a lesson.

22

Morengáru lay facedown on the floor of his hut, staring into the fire. Vague shapes seemed to loom in the curling smoke. When the misty shapes became clearer, he thought he recognized the young men who had come to fetch him. *Morans*. And he remembered, with a longing so strong it hurt, his last day with the Masai.

The day of the lion.

He was only an *olaiyoni*, a boy who still had to earn his *moran* spear. Each one of the spear bearers who came to get

68

him had already killed a lion, and some of them proudly carried the scars to prove it. That morning they were bright and excited. It was like a holiday for them; instead of having to watch the cattle, they could go and help Morengáru find his lion.

They came running through the dewy grass, all about the same age, and all wearing long loincloths the same ocher-brown as their skin. Their long hair, stiff with dried mud, was the same color. Their hair knots swung rhythmically against their shoulders. They could all have been brothers, tall and handsome with narrow noses, and teeth shining white and strong in the light of the early sun.

They jostled and pushed each other the way only real Masai would, companionable and carefree. They would never touch him, the half-Kikuyu, that way. That morning, Morengáru had been more aware of the difference than ever. They had come to help him. They would even risk their lives for him, but only because the law of the tribe required it. That was when he had decided to leave—if he survived. He was determined to show the Masai he was a match for any of them, and then he would go his own way.

Like athletes, the *morans* ran effortlessly through the grass, their silhouettes slim against a sky streaked with rosy color. They disturbed a hare, and when the animal zigzagged away, they went after it. Laughing and shrieking, they spread out over the hill. They ran as fast as they could, their long legs stretching with an ease that was a delight to see. They managed to catch the hare, held the terrified animal up triumphantly, then put it back on the ground. They returned, laughing, to Morengáru.

Morengáru stood waiting, motionless. Behind him he heard the familiar morning sounds of the village waking.

69

Women went to fetch water, taking their children with them to bathe. Old men crept, coughing, from their smoky huts and sat in the rising sun to warm their weary bones. Cocks crowed the way they crow the world over. And hens took dust baths, cackling loudly. It was a morning no different from any other, except for him, Morengáru.

From the moment the lion had first made itself heard, Morengáru had known this would be his lion. It had been a new experience, lying awake at night, listening to the roaring of the lion you were going to kill the next day.

Molo had been appointed to lead the hunt. This was a bit of luck for Morengáru. Molo had successfully conducted many lion hunts. He was the proud owner of a whole string of claws, and that spoke for itself. Even the lion's terrifying teeth were less feared than the claws high on the inside of its forepaws. These claws were at least four inches long, hard as steel, curved like a sickle, and razor-sharp. Most of the time they were invisible, retracted inside the skin. But when they were extended, at a right angle, one single stroke could turn your belly inside out.

Molo had been given those claws by grateful *morans*, who knew only too well that without his experience and tactics they might have stayed behind on the plain, dead. No wonder Molo looked so sure of himself. Morengáru, calmly greeting his helpers, hoped he too created such a fearless impression.

But if he managed to fool others, he couldn't deceive himself. He was afraid. And every time he thought back to the night before, his fear grew. It meant nothing, he kept telling himself. It had only been a nightmare. You're awake now. Forget it. But he knew better. It hadn't been a dream, because he hadn't been asleep. All night.

Just as he had been about to fall asleep, a sound had startled him, and he had spent the rest of the night wide awake, listening. For the first time in his life, he had felt fear. Even now, in the clear morning light, that gnawing in his stomach continued, as if he was being slowly hollowed out. It had started when he heard the lion roar, out there in the boundless night. It was such a heavy sound, booming far and wide, unimpeded by any walls. And it seemed like a lonely lion. Too ill-tempered and self-centered to live in a group. Morengáru had not been afraid when he heard that roar. On the contrary, he had even looked forward to the morning. But a little later he'd heard the rasping cough of the lion. That's when he had sat up straight, his eyes wide open.

Unlikely though it seemed, the sound of the coughing carried at least as far as the roar, it was so deep and hoarse, and went on for so long. Perhaps the lion's roar didn't sound really threatening because you knew it was meant to. But then why did that deep coughing in the night sound so sinister? It was only the ugly, breathless, raw coughing of an old lion. Or of an old man.

It had to be. Senteu had come back to life. Senteu, his Masai grandfather, who had been the terror of his childhood. Senteu, that malicious old man, hideously maimed by a lion, paralyzed but still vigorous enough to terrorize a whole family. Too many nights the little boy Morengáru had lain listening to the wheezy cough from that squashed rib cage, keeping still for fear his grandfather would notice he was awake and send him off into the night to fetch water, fresh water from the river. Time and again, that fearful journey over the dark plain, followed by the creeping shadows of hyenas and wild dogs . . .

His father had never protected him from the cruel old

71

man. And his mother had had no influence at all. It had taken years before one night the old man was seized by such a bad fit of coughing that he didn't get over it. Years.

Last night, Senteu had once again uttered his hoarse cough, and instantly Morengáru had become that tormented child again; keeping still, listening in the darkness. And although these images—like any dream, no matter how terrifying—had faded away in the first sunlight, his fear had not.

But the others needn't know what was going on inside him. They only knew he was a reckless young man and that it was high time he won his *moran* spear. Silently, Morengáru walked on with the *morans*, into the dew-covered grassland.

In order to make it easier to move, he took off his only garment and folded it around his left arm. In his right hand he held his spear. They found the lion's spoor easily and followed it. The lion had killed a zebra in the night and had dragged his prey quite a way so he could eat his fill somewhere sheltered. Molo predicted they would find him asleep in the shade, too sluggish to get away. And so it was. Only an hour later they found his hiding place, in among the impenetrable thornbushes.

They threw stones randomly until an angry growl told them exactly where the lion was. Then the throwing started in earnest. Not long after, the thorny branches shook violently.

To their amazement, the lion emerged calmly. He strode away through the tall grass, without deigning to glance at his attackers. Stunned, the young men stared after him. But the lion's dignity was diminished by the ridiculous way his overfull belly swung from side to side as he walked. When Morengáru saw him haughtily walk away with that sagging belly nearly dragging along the ground, he burst out laughing. And instantly he felt his old fighting spirit return. With a piercing yell he started running to cut the lion off. As if coming out of a trance, the *morans* started moving too, waving their spears, shouting to attract the beast's attention. Molo yelled instructions, and the boys spread out over the plain. The hunt was on, and could only end in one way.

Full of renewed self-confidence, Morengáru waited for the lion, his spear raised. But the animal still showed no sign of fear. He looked as if he was annoyed by this commotion, just when he felt like a peaceful sleep. The *morans* who had cut him off were jumping up and down, challenging and whooping with shrill voices. And, indeed, the lion turned back.

For a moment he stood there, stretched to his full length, his great head turned toward Morengáru. The morning breeze made his mane stand out like a wide collar. He growled discontentedly, and then, with a sound that seemed to come from deep inside his chest, he started coughing.

And Morengáru's challenging shout changed into a whimper. The others looked at him in surprise.

23

Crouched in the dark outside Morengáru's hut, the young Kikuyu *nyama* and his friend weren't too sure what to do. Inside, the half-Masai lay sleeping off his drunkenness, that was clear. What could they do to give him the fright of his life?

The rising moon came to their aid. The white glow slowly

creeping across the yard lit the spotted leopard skin. That magnificent pelt, which had produced such great rewards for Morengáru, hung drying on a rack, high up out of the reach of hyenas. Occasionally, the fur moved in the wind, and the wide open mouth with the great fangs still looked terrifying. It may have been the effect of the moonlight, but even in death the leopard seemed to shake with murderous fury.

The *nyama* and his friend crept silently to the rack and pulled down the leopard skin. They grinned at each other. The joke was so obvious they didn't need any words.

24

The lion being herded toward Morengáru by the *morans* was a sorry-looking specimen. Not only had his mane been ruined by the thorns, but he had bald patches all over his body. He was an old, mangy lion, his skin of no value. But there was nothing wrong with his teeth and claws.

The lion was getting annoyed with being harassed. He didn't want to fight, but neither did he want to flee over the hot plain. He wanted to lie down in the shade, to digest the meat he had devoured. But wherever he turned, that shouting kept coming at him. He couldn't understand what it meant.

Of course he couldn't understand, for though he was no longer young, in all his long life he hadn't learned the meaning of fear. From the wrinkled tip of his nose to the black plume at the end of his tail, he measured no less than 8 feet ten inches. And he weighed at least five hundred and fifty pounds. This lion was aware of his superiority and walked through the grass as if he had no doubt about who was master.

The *morans* were not misled by his apparent lethargy. They knew about that. They knew his inert mood could turn in an instant. At a safe distance they formed a tight semicircle around him, staying well hidden in the tall grass. They took care not to lose sight of the lion for a moment. Even if they couldn't actually see him, they kept their eyes fixed in his direction. Even when they bent to pick up stones. Even when they shouted details of his movements to each other. Every rustle in the grass could mean a sudden attack by the lion.

Shouting and hurling stones, they kept driving the lion on from bush to bush, laughing at his growing irritation. It was almost as if they could see right into his wild heart, so quickly did they react to his movements. He didn't understand what was happening to him. The simple truth still had to penetrate his fearless lion's brain. Only then would there be an end to this game of torment, an end as sudden as it was bloody.

The lion flattened his ears and thrashed the ground with his tail. Hindered by his full belly, he started walking again. He wanted to lie down, his head flat on his forelegs and his eyes shut tightly against the flies. But every time he did, the shouting started again and stones rained down on his body. Confused, he shook his heavy head. What was the meaning of this? It didn't occur to him that his pursuers were after a real fight. He had never been seriously challenged, except, of course, by other lions.

For the first time, the lion stopped without immediately lying down. He looked over his shoulder and gave a warning roar. It was an awe-inspiring sound, meant to create an impression. It started somewhere deep down in his chest, like a dull rumble, rapidly grew in volume, and finally filled the air with an ear-splitting noise. And while he roared, the lion watched for the effect of his performance.

His pursuers seemed unimpressed. Once more, the lion shook the air with his mighty roar. This time, scornful laughter and another hail of stones greeted his warning. His giant mouth slammed shut, and for a moment he looked almost taken aback. He turned to face the *morans*, as if he had finally decided they deserved his attention. He raised his dark mane, and suddenly he looked twice as big, and no longer ridiculous at all. Then he walked on.

Again his whooping, running tormenters cut him off. Angered, he looked the other way. There, he could see only a single one of these creatures. Motionless. Silent. Obviously he would walk in that direction, but deep in his hunter's heart he didn't like it. He found this silent waiting much more threatening than all the noise. And with good reason, although, of course, the lion couldn't know this. The single man meant real danger for him, for that man had to earn his *moran* spear.

Morengáru rested his spear far back on his right shoulder, ready to thrust with all his strength. From the movements he could work out that the lion was getting ready to attack. You couldn't mistake it: the way the rolling muscles under the brown-yellow skin were suddenly visible. The way the tail was stretched out straight, trembling along its whole length. The way the enormous head moved lower and lower, until the bloodstained old man's beard nearly brushed the ground. . . . The attack would happen with such lightning speed that you wouldn't see much more than a yellow flash in the shaking grass.

The lion started moving, but nowhere near as fast as he could. Instead of attacking, he tried to reach the bushes. But the *morans* got there first. Their voices echoed through the morning air as they overtook the lion with long leaps. Molo warned them not to get too close. The lion might attack them instead of Morengáru. That warning was timely, for the boys were beside themselves with excitement. They became more and more rash, radiant at their own recklessness. Only Morengáru stood waiting silently. And so, finally, the lion turned around. All at once, without any threatening display, he sprinted toward the solitary man.

Instantly, the memory of the crippled Senteu disappeared. The lion came storming at him with astonishing speed. Morengáru braced himself. But the lion was just bluffing. At the last moment he changed direction. He still felt no urge to fight. Without slowing down, he tried to find a gap in the ring of *morans*. Soon he would discover that there was only one way to break through that circle, and then each hunter would face the moment of truth. All ten of them stood prepared, tense, the sun sparkling on the metal tips of their quivering spears.

Suddenly the lion slowed. Two or three times his tail thumped the grass, and then his enormous body lifted itself as if weightless. But the thud when he landed betrayed his five hundred and fifty pounds. His shaggy body brushed past one of the *morans*, who was hurled aside without his spear making contact. The others clacked their tongues disapprovingly. They were disappointed at the lion's lack of fighting spirit and at the slow reaction of their mate. Now they had to start the pursuit all over again. The lion took cover among the thick thornbushes, and it wouldn't be easy to get him out of there.

Somewhere deep inside the tangle of thorny branches the hunted lion made a rasping noise. Not to frighten his attackers, but because he couldn't see a way out. And on hearing that ugly, wheezy cough, Morengáru was paralyzed again. He stood rigid when the lion broke out of the scrub right near him. In full sunlight, the lion paused for a single moment, looking at him, and Morengáru didn't use his spear. The next instant, the lion was running past him.

The *moran* who stood in the lion's path realized that threatening shouts would not work. The beast would no longer let itself be scared away. Without any hesitation, he hurled his spear and hit the attacking lion in the side of the head. Again, the lion did not follow the familiar pattern: instead of countering attack with attack, he clawed frantically at the spear. Growling, he twisted round until he managed to wrench the weapon out. Meanwhile, the *moran* had drawn his *simi*, a broad knife, twenty inches long. Not that you could do much with that against the teeth and claws of a furious lion.

In that one moment when the *moran* understood he was at the mercy of the attacking animal, he looked across to Morengáru. It was a look full of contempt. The half-Kikuyu had done nothing when he had had his chance. Now someone else had to pay for his cowardice. Face to face with certain death, the Masai had only one thought: He would have to die for the sake of this worthless Kikuyu. He had no time to think about death itself—no time for fear or regret— but he did have time for that one look.

Morengáru felt that look as if something powerful had struck him.

The lion hurled himself at the young man. With a single lash of his right foreleg he sent his *simi* flying into the air. Then he tried to drag the *moran* closer. But before he could manage, something happened that the Masai would talk about for a long time to come.

Morengáru started to move.

The contemptuous look of the *moran* had unleashed the most violent emotion he had ever felt. It was as if everything inside him bunched up: all those years of loneliness, of incomprehension and contempt, and all the hatred from the past. The hatred of that hoarse coughing in the night, the malicious persecutor of his childhood. All that pent-up emotion finally burst out in an explosion of fury and fighting spirit. With the blazing look of a fanatic who can think of only one thing, he ran straight at the lion, throwing away his spear as he ran.

The lion held the *moran* down with his weight, but before he could inflict his fatal bite, he was distracted by another man. He raised his huge head, his lips drawn back in a snarl.

Morengáru seemed to see nothing, hear nothing. He kept coming at the lion. Meanwhile, the *moran* tried to wriggle out from underneath, distracting his attention. That was the moment Morengáru reached the lion.

As if it was the only thing to do, Morengáru grasped the lion by the tail. He hung on, not by the black tuft at the end but right next to the root of the tail, for everyone knows how a lion can stiffen his tail and sweep you out of the way with it. And so he carried out the legendary act the Masai call *melombuki*, because he had no idea what else he could do.

Melombuki. Grasping a lion by the tail and hanging on until the others come to your assistance with their spears and *simis*. In all of the Loita there were perhaps two people alive who had dared do something like this, and their names were known in every settlement. No one could give a more convincing demonstration of courage. But Morengáru wasn't trying to demonstrate anything. He just wanted to pull the lion away

79

from the *moran* who had looked at him so contemptuously; to undo what had been his fault.

His face rigid with stubborn fury, he hung on to the lion's tail. The infuriated lion reared up and swung around. But already he was surrounded on all sides. Yelling with excitement, the *morans* hacked at the lion with their knives and long spears. Blood spattered everywhere. The lion dug his broad paws into the ground so he could hurl himself forward with more force, and Morengáru did the same to brace himself. He was dragged quite a way. The lion spun around, flailing his forelegs, but the very movement put Morengáru out of his reach. No matter how he was hurled about, Morengáru kept hanging onto the tail.

Several *morans* sustained deep wounds in their shoulders and arms, but by now they were so excited they could hardly feel pain. The lion had raged and roared, but eventually could only croak as he choked on his own blood. But his voice was drowned out by the wild shouts of the *morans* and the slashing sound of sharp metal.

It was over in a flash. The lion sank to the ground, pierced with spears. His head was hacked to pieces. In their frenzy, the *morans* kept stabbing until all that was left of their arch-enemy was a bloody mass. And then the plain became still. Morengáru lay in the grass, still hanging on to the tail. He was in a trance. The amazing thing was that he had suffered no injury whatsoever. He was unaware that he had won a glorious title. The *morans* didn't allow themselves the time to examine their wounds. They crowded around Morengáru, shaking their hair knots, calling his name. Molo cut off the tail with his *simi* when he saw that Morengáru wasn't going to let go of it.

"*Melombuki,*" he said with awe. "*Melombuki.*"

And the others repeated that word in chorus, ever more loudly and rhythmically. They danced toward Morengáru, clapping their hands in time, singing in deep voices, from down in their chests. It was a savage song, beginning with a low growling and ending with a roar. They surrounded him, the new *melombuki*, and sang and danced their famed lion dance for him.

25

Morengáru was wakened abruptly out of the savage dream about the killing of his lion. Then, in that unguarded moment—a single moment of confusion, madness, and blind fury—he performed the fatal act that was to change the direction of his life forever. To the Kikuyu it made no difference whether he acted deliberately or in all innocence, whether he was sober or drunk—in their eyes the only thing that counted was the disastrous result.

The young *nyama* and his friend had only meant to give Morengáru a good fright. They slipped into his *shamba* and brought the dead leopard back to life. They made the wide mouth, full of glittering teeth, float up to Morengáru, growling and hissing as convincingly as they could, ready to run away laughing at the first reaction. But they weren't prepared for such an extreme response. They didn't know the wild heart of the hunter.

What could Morengáru think when he saw the leopard's head coming at him out of the darkness, so close and true to life? He was being attacked! There was no time for doubt.

Like everyone who lives in the wilderness, he had learned to trust his first impulse. He reacted without thinking, without hesitating. Instead of sitting up, rigid with fear, the way others might, he shot up and in the same movement grasped his *moran* spear. Hidden under the leopard skin, the *nyama* was pierced by the long metal point before he could even utter a sound. He was pinned to the mud floor, and his friend fled, screaming with horror.

There stood Morengáru. He wasn't even quite awake, and couldn't make sense of what had happened. Incredulously, he listened to the labored breathing of the *nyama* bleeding to death under the leopard skin. Slowly it began to dawn on him that a great calamity had befallen him.

PART 3

the wanderer's fire

26

He whose fire remains lonely
is an unfortunate man.

—KIKUYU SAYING

He had lived with the Kikuyu long enough not to have
false hopes, but he was still surprised by his sentence. Why?
Wasn't it obvious the Council would grab this chance to put
him in his place?

Notions of "mitigating circumstances" or "acting in self-
defense" were not known to the Kikuyu. The how and why
of a crime were never considered. He who took a life had to
compensate for a life. Whether the killing was deliberate or
not made no difference: He had robbed a family of a son.
The trial was not about guilt or innocence, but about price:
an endless bickering about how much the compensation
should amount to.

The sentence of the Council would be binding. "Right of
appeal" didn't exist. A person who didn't accept his sentence
was ostracized and ceased to exist for his neighbors. He
would no longer be welcome even in the faraway villages on
the other side of the Ngong.

What had been the dead *nyama*'s value? How great a loss
had his family suffered through his untimely death? That

question could be argued forever, and those old men had plenty of time. What the parents could have expected from this son was examined at length. Even if he had been useless all his life, through his death he would bring a small fortune to his family. Didn't the murderer own two cows?

Morengáru saw them sitting opposite each other: the members of the Council and the representatives of the family, patiently absorbed in argument. He waited without hope. The meeting went on for three days, and everyone in the village felt involved. It was a constant topic of conversation. He could almost hear the old men commenting gleefully: Here was a typical example of youthful overconfidence leading to disaster! His unexpected wealth had been a thorn in the flesh for many. Now the Council would make sure he was as poor as he had been before. He was certain he would lose his two cows, although that would be incredibly high compensation, considering it was not a case of an eldest son, or even an only child on whom the parents would have to depend in their old age. Despite this, the Council was most willing to listen to the representatives. All their arguments were repeated with a knowing smile in the *shambas*, like so many clever moves in a game everybody wanted to enjoy.

At first Morengáru had felt remorse and compassion for his victim's parents. He had listened to their lament the morning they carried their dead child into the hills, where they were greeted by the distant laughter of hyenas. But these feelings soon changed to bitterness. The family hired no fewer than three representatives, all famed advocates, who would be entitled to a share of the compensation. The three of them had not only climbed up to the *boma* to inspect his cows but also checked out his hut to see what could be got there. Morengáru had felt like the fattened goat.

Throughout the deliberations a wide circle of listeners murmured agreement at the end of every speech.

"This whole performance has only one object," Morengáru said scornfully to Kupanya, who had come to visit him. "They want to skin me alive."

Mauro kept the situation under control with ease. To outsiders, this had to appear a fair trial. His speeches were slow and dignified, with many pauses for thought—a luxury he could afford: No one would interrupt him and everyone hung on his words.

Meanwhile, the murdered *nyama*'s reputation as a model son grew by the minute. But not once were the three representatives challenged. The dead man was presented as a tireless worker, a vigilant shepherd, full of care for his parents and an example to his brothers. His proposed marriage—which no one had known about, but which no one doubted!—would have forged a close alliance with neighbors who were very rich and had no sons.

If Mauro enjoyed the situation, he didn't show it. Occasionally he even surprised his audience by mentioning something in Morengáru's favor. And when the verdict was finally about to be pronounced, he interrupted the session to sacrifice a goat at his own expense so the entrails could be consulted. The spirits of the ancestors had to guide him to a just sentence.

Nice old Mauro, thought Morengáru, wasn't this clever! While the bleating of the dying goat could be heard through the village, the whole meeting waited, looking serious. Morengáru gazed around the circle. No one would meet his eye. Not one of these powerful men had enough character to return his challenging glance. These elders were supposed to be the wisest men of the tribe, but they were only the wealthiest. It was bad enough to be bled dry, but it was even worse that it was done by judges he couldn't possibly respect.

27

Morengáru had never expected understanding from the village elders. Yet these were the same men who had seen his mother follow her Masai husband from the village. They must have suspected how sold-out and betrayed she felt. Or had these Wise Ones, who now so studiously avoided his eyes, also managed to be looking the other way when she turned for the last time to the green gardens of her youth?

Once more Morengáru scanned the row of earnest faces. The sun shone into their empty eyes. Meanwhile, Mauro was still absent. Why was it taking so long? Would the great *mundumugu*, this time of all times, be unable to see a clear sign from the gods? Suddenly, Morengáru wished desperately for the end of this performance. Mauro would have the last word, whatever happened.

One of the old men said philosophically, as if trying to allay the others' impatience, "Of course, we must always strive for insight and reason, particularly when it is our task to sit in judgment upon a fellow human being, but we must not overlook the fact that arguments can never prevail over the word of the medicine man. Does not the light of the human spirit pale in the blazing light of divine revelation, as the moon pales when the sun rises?"

This is as good as a judgment, Morengáru thought. Those words give Mauro a free hand.

The patriarch returned to the circle, wiping his hands clean. He blinked his beady eyes against the bright daylight and solemnly donned his monkey-fur cap. For a short while he sat whispering with the other members of the Council. The white monkey-fur fringe shook with his every movement. There was much nodding of heads, the faces inscrutable. Then he addressed the representatives of the bereaved family.

Morengáru was only half listening. He tried not to look at Mauro's self-satisfied face. He stared over the reed roofs of the village to the ancient bare hills. Oh, to lie down under a mimosa tree somewhere out there and sleep, he thought, surprising himself.

Mauro's copper armbands jingled as he pointed his staff at the sorrowful parents, simple little people, almost hidden behind their representatives. He spoke to them, full of compassion, and offered them Morengáru's cows as compensation for the death of their son. They listened with shining eyes, their lips silently shaping his words, as if repeating them to make quite sure—those incredible words offering them a fortune.

The solemnity of the occasion dictated that everyone remain silent, but all around you could hear deep sighs of emotion. The three representatives nodded at each other, satisfied: Their efforts had seldom been so well rewarded. The Council members whispered together excitedly, as if the sentence had come as a surprise to them. Mauro's eyes revealed nothing. No triumph, no gloating, no pity, nothing.

He had taken away Morengáru's proud possession. But

that wasn't enough. Mauro hadn't played his trump card yet. Everyone assumed the session of the court was over—everyone, except Mauro and his victim. Morengáru felt that Mauro had something else in mind. And whatever it was, no matter how fatal a blow, he was not going to let it take him by surprise. He waited, not even blinking.

Mauro took his time. He kept talking in that whining tone, choosing his words carefully. Because he used so many old-fashioned expressions, it all sounded highly formal, and Morengáru had trouble following him. The others were familiar with his outdated language and with the customary formulas for ending such a session. But it was the first time Morengáru had heard this speech. And when its significance penetrated his mind, he knew Grandpa Mauro had won.

Morengáru heard that from then on he was forbidden to enter the village. He had to be gone by nightfall. He was banished. Forever. This was no surprise to the others. They knew it was not a real banishment. It was just one of those formalities. You didn't actually have to leave the village. All you had to do was formally express your remorse and ask for the sentence of banishment to be set aside. And the same ancient tradition ensured that your request would be granted. Every Kikuyu knew this. It was the traditional way of concluding a sitting of the court. There were plenty of people ready to explain this to Morengáru. Obligingly they crowded round him, but he listened stony-faced. It was as if he couldn't understand, as if he couldn't possibly comprehend the idea. He just sat there, staring at Mauro.

How cunningly the old man had played his game! Nobody could accuse him of malice, but he had succeeded in maneuvering his hated grandson out of his life forever. He had foreseen exactly what was going to happen. To the dismay of the bystanders, Morengáru refused to ask for his banishment to be revoked. Again they explained it was a mere formality. It meant nothing; it was just a matter of procedure. But Morengáru remained silent.

Mauro had seen the situation accurately. No Masai, not even a half-Masai, would ever beg for mercy. So he used a half-forgotten Kikuyu tradition as his king hit. Morengáru refused to join in what had become a ceremonial game, so the ancient rule regained its full force. Everyone looked at Morengáru who, like a real *moran*, threw his head back and returned their stares with the fearless—but not all that clever—look of the lion killer in his eyes. Then the old man knew his ruse had worked. He could barely control his glee. It radiated from his black eyes.

Morengáru understood perfectly what his grandfather was up to. His banishment could only take effect because he himself upheld the sentence. It was as cunning as it was simple. He knew he was playing into Mauro's hands. But he couldn't do otherwise. He preferred to leave the village with his head held high. He had lost. The fight, with all its tricks and schemes, was over, and the loser had to clear the field. No mercy asked or given. Silently grandfather and grandson exchanged a final glance. Then Morengáru got up and strode out of the circle.

28

A small group accompanied Morengáru along the path through the gardens and out to the hills. Kariuki played a homemade instrument, a couple of strings stretched across a hollowed-out gourd. He didn't sing, but the soft, mournful tones told clearly how he felt. Bajabi and Kiribai walked along, and Kimani, unusually quiet, and of course Kupanya, crying openly and shamelessly. Fortunately it was getting dark.

Morengáru could hardly distinguish their faces. Only the white of their eyes was visible. When they reached the last of the gardens, he said, "No farther. You have to go back."

"Tell us where you're going, so we can come and see you," Bajabi shouted.

"You're not allowed to visit a person who's been banished, you know that. And anyway, I've no idea where I'm going. You just go back. It'll be pitch dark soon."

"But what about you?" Kupanya sobbed.

"I don't get lost easily. I know a good camping spot a bit farther on. Don't worry about me."

In the end it was the unpredictable Kariuki who took the lead. He started playing a song they all recognized. A defiant song he had made up himself one stormy night when he had been lost. That's why it was called "The Shouting Song." Despite everything, Morengáru had to laugh. "Well done, Kariuki," he called. "You take them home."

So, playing and singing, Kariuki marched back along the path. The others followed hesitantly. Only Kupanya didn't move.

"Shall I come with you, Morengáru?" he asked, against his better judgment.

"Why don't you go home now, and we'll meet up tomorrow."

"How shall I find you?"

"If you get up before dawn, you'll see a big fire. That's where I'll be."

"Agreed," said Kupanya, and stopped sobbing.

They both knew it was not a real arrangement. Even if Kupanya got up early to look out over the dark plain, Morengáru would take good care that no fire was burning. But it was easier to say good-bye this way.

Morengáru walked away quickly. He heard Kariuki's shrill music fade behind him. Kupanya shouted something, but his voice blew away in the wind. Morengáru did not look back. It was over. His stay with the Kikuyu had come to an end.

29

In the first morning light, it looked as if a grass fire was raging in the east. But it was only the rising sun. Morengáru stretched. He was so stiff he could hear his muscles creak. He peered over the treeless plain, but it was still too dark to distinguish anything. Geese flew overhead. He stared after them as far as the hazy edge of the savanna. There, two antelopes were grazing, tall and gray in the dawning light. Morengáru's gaze roved farther. Suddenly he said with a scornful laugh, "Look who's here."

A solitary oryx came galloping over the plain. He appeared smaller than Morengáru remembered, but his single horn was clearly visible. It had to be the same one. The one-horned bull. Morengáru watched him for a long time, shaking his head. The oryx kept running purposefully past quietly grazing animals, until he finally seemed to dissolve into the red sky.

When Morengáru started walking, he had no clear idea where he was going. For the moment, he traveled northeast. That's where the oryx must be heading, for its tracks led in a remarkably straight line in that direction.

As he walked, Morengáru pondered his options. There weren't too many for a man who had grown up in the open spaces of the highlands. The extensive grasslands belonged to the nomads and their cattle, and they wouldn't welcome a destitute wanderer. Past the grasslands, the desert began: nothing but saltpans and sandstorms, the home of the Somali, a race possibly even more proud and intolerant than the Masai. And farther north, in the Danakil desert, lived the notorious Avari. They apparently still kept to the old custom of murdering strangers to protect their scarce water supplies. The west and south were strictly Masai territory, so there was nothing for him that way. And farther on?

Farther on lived a few dispersed small tribes. You couldn't really call them proper tribes. Groups without leaders, without laws. Paupers. He wouldn't take up with people like that. He would prefer to be on his own. So there weren't many choices. But he might think of something later.

He was in no hurry, and for the moment didn't feel lonely. Fury crowded out all other feelings. Fury at having been robbed and driven away. He would rather spend the rest of his life by himself than ever go back. They'd have a long wait!

But that night, as he lay listening to the crazy laughter of a hyena, he was surprised to find that he did feel utterly lonely and desolate. Not that he had anything to fear, but still . . . *fisi*'s loud laughter sounded so self-assured, somehow knowing, as if that eater of corpses were saying: Your turn will come, and sooner than you think.

Did the hyena know from experience that every solitary man in the wilderness would sooner or later be his? Was that why he waited patiently at a distance, chuckling and shaking his head?

Morengáru wondered if he was really doomed; beyond hope from the moment he started out on his lonely adventure. Was that how it would end? Was the night close when nothing would be left of his thoughts and dreams? Would all that disappear irrevocably in the jaws of "the shadow that waits patiently"?

The morning light drove away his somber mood. His good spirits returned. No use thinking that far ahead. Serves no purpose. For the time being, he would keep walking northeast. There was supposed to be plenty of game there. A legendary hunters' paradise.

Sometimes he took a group of gazelles by surprise. They would stretch their necks, pricking up their ears to discover the source of sudden, silent death that had overtaken one of them. Most animals reacted too slowly to his appearance. Herds of restless wildebeest only really started moving once they sniffed his scent. Then they would thunder away, disappearing behind a great cloud of dust.

Morengáru moved on, without plan, without purpose. He lost count of the days. From morning to night he kept going, a lonely wanderer in a landscape of hills that all looked the same. Yet one morning he realized that the landscape was nothing like the green highland of the Ngong, nor like the treeless plain of the Loita. Low, rounded mounds stretched away endlessly ahead of him in long lines, the tops bristly with thorns, the sides covered in seemingly lifeless scrub.

The air here was hot and dry because the wind brought the heat from the easterly desert. When he was lucky enough to find some rainwater in one of the numerous holes, it was brackish and so muddy he had to filter it through a piece of cloth before he could drink it. But for Morengáru that was no reason to look for water in a different direction.

Thousands of zebras wandered in tightly packed herds in this undulating landscape, seeking safety in numbers from extensive families of lions. But they showed no fear of Morengáru; they did not know that humans are the most dangerous hunters on earth. In his turn, Morengáru was not afraid of the lions. It was simply not in their nature to attack a human unprovoked.

At the end of every day, Morengáru sat by his fire, staring at the endless procession of silhouettes moving across the low red sun. One herd followed the other, forever seeking water and grass and safety. Even the sun sometimes disappeared behind the dust they kicked up; then they seemed to be moving through a red fog. And as he sat watching those massive herds, Morengáru tried not to think of that single, solitary animal that had, like him, left the safety of its herd. The oryx.

Why he kept following its track was a riddle he preferred not to think about. He shook off any thought of the oryx itself. The track was simply there. And what difference did it make, anyway, where he walked? Staying made no more sense than going on. But staying meant inaction. And inaction meant thinking about his situation.

And if, sooner or later, he did overtake the oryx, then what? There was no sense pursuing an animal you didn't want to kill. The flesh would be inedible, and the hide not worth the bother. Pursued or not, One-horn was safe from him.

One-horn. That was what he had been calling the oryx lately. And that in itself was ridiculous. A name you gave to a friend or an enemy, but the oryx was neither. He was just following its tracks, that was all. Morengáru didn't even want to catch up with him. And yet—without those tracks his existence would have seemed pointless.

Every morning it took more effort to get up. Why not stay where he was, lying by the cold remains of his fire? Who or what would make him go on? Now that his fury had abated, all that was left was a feeling of abandonment. And homesickness.

Sadly he realized that he would never know if Kupanya ever gained the recognition as a healer he had so long deserved. And that he would never spend another evening listening to Kariuki's melancholy music, or Kimani's uninhibited ravings. Evenings like that were gone forever. And he would never witness Bajabi and Kiribai marrying their lovely *bibis*. He had forfeited his chance of a Kikuyu life. And his time in the Ngong was past. For good. He was doomed to a life of loneliness and exile, to a mere barbaric hunter's existence.

But a human was not meant to be alone. Even though he was used to being by himself, it had never been real loneliness, only a separation you could undo simply by going back to people. A human being needed company, someone to talk to, friends. Gone. For good. He belonged nowhere any more, had no one to go back to.

Gradually, he felt that his solitariness was beginning to change him. It was as if he was slowly becoming less human and more like the animals around him. Get up, eat, wander on, sleep—it was just an existence, not a life.

My only friend, he sometimes thought bitterly, is *fisi*. He

97

is always ready for me. He faithfully keeps me company. If the morning ever comes when getting up is no longer worth the bother, *fisi* will not let me down.

More and more often Morengáru found himself staring over the hills, vaguely wishing he was dead. Now this only lasted a few moments, but one day the feeling might not go away, and then he wouldn't get up and *fisi* would have his way. But things hadn't got that far yet. Every day his fighting spirit returned with the light. And then the trail of the oryx was waiting.

In places it wasn't much more than a shallow hoof print, a snapped branch, or a flattened blade of grass, but for Morengáru the trail was as clear as a path. Without it, he would probably be wandering about in circles, but now it led him in a straight line to the horizon. Day after day. It had become his only hold on reality; everything else was fading.

All the same, where the oryx was heading so determinedly was a mystery to Morengáru. The animal never seemed to hesitate, never drifted off course. You would almost think that something was waiting for him there, beyond all those hills that repeated themselves, like mirror images, as far as the shimmering horizon.

It became a routine. He covered roughly the same distance every day, through a landscape in which one day's walk was nothing, it was so changeless. And every night he lay by his fire in a spot that was in every way like the one where he had slept the night before. Looking up at the stars, which seemed to jump at him out of the dark, he was sometimes overwhelmed by a black depression. Then he could feel his friend *fisi*'s all-knowing look turned on him in the dark, and he would angrily shake his head. Not yet, you ugly corpse-eater! Often, when he could feel such a black mood coming over him, he would jump up and start to sing, loudly and defiantly, "The Shouting Song":

Are you there? Show me where!
I'm sick of standing here!
This is no game!
Morengáru is my name!

30

He awoke with the uneasy feeling that something had happened. Quickly he looked around, but nothing had changed. It took a while for him to realize that something had happened, not in his surroundings but inside him.

To his amazement, he heard himself say, "One-horn must die."

That frightened him. Why must it happen? Who had decided? He sat up straight. Around him the dawn light seemed to get darker in waves, instead of brighter. But he knew that was only the hills looming in the first light. More and more shapes, vague and one-dimensional, surrounded him while he sat shivering. The fire had almost burned out, just a couple of charred branches still smoldered. It would be a while before the sun gave any real warmth. Better go and find some more firewood. While he was occupied with that, he said again, without any obvious reason, "One-horn must die."

At first he tried hard to think of something else, but he couldn't. What sense could it possibly make to kill One-horn? "It has to be," said the voice in his head. It was his own voice, but clearer and more distinct than his speaking voice.

Nonsense, Morengáru thought, shrugging.

"That is what has been decided," said the voice.

A ludicrous decision, Morengáru felt. And who might have made this decision?

"You."

"Not me," said Morengáru, shaking his head.

He returned to his camp carrying an armful of wood, and turned his full attention to restarting the fire. Without realizing, he grinned cunningly into the blaze. He had outsmarted the voice.

The fire started to warm him, and he relaxed. Strange how certain thoughts could suddenly come up in your mind, as if they had been lying in wait, fully formed, in your head. Usually they were mad brainwaves, as unpredictable as an arrow flying wildly off target; and sometimes as dangerous, like that time he burst out laughing in the middle of a ceremony. Everybody was angry with him, and he tried to explain that he hadn't meant to be disrespectful, tears of laughter streaming down his cheeks.

"From now on, you can laugh out loud about any joke that comes into your head. Nobody will be disturbed by it," Morengáru said. He sighed, shaking his head to drive that thought away.

But hadn't it always been like that? He always had conflicting thoughts about anything he did. He had envied the Masai boys their straightforwardness and tried to be like that himself, suppressing the questions that bothered him and undermined his certainty again and again. How he had envied them their peace of mind, their clear and simple opinions. Pushing back second thoughts and doubts, how could he ever sound as convincing as they did? Ambiguities didn't exist for them, and complexity they proudly dismissed. Stuff for Kikuyus, they laughed. So he had always kept his thoughts to himself.

"All that no longer matters."

Morengáru stood up and watched the day break. One burst of birdsong followed another, but all that lively activity didn't cheer him up. He felt smaller and more insignificant than he ever had, alone in the wilderness. His existence counted for nothing.

"One-horn must die," the voice in his head said again.

He couldn't help jumping with fright. The voice was so clear and so full of authority. Never before had a thought so taken over his consciousness. It was like a thought with its own will, its own voice. A Masai thought! Had the Masai in him finally woken up? The true Masai, not enfeebled by Kikuyu blood? The doubt-free thinker of the single thought, the dreamer of the single dream? And was it the cunning Kikuyu in him who tried to ignore the voice, playing deaf, seeking refuge in ambiguities?

Morengáru sighed. He stared wide-eyed into the flames, trying to remember if anything special had happened that night—something that might explain why he had woken up with this particular thought. But the past night was like all nights before it, just as this particular hill was like all the other hills. And yet last night this one idea had hatched in his brain like a cuckoo egg in the wrong nest.

"One-horn must die. That is what has been decided."

Not a decision he had made. And yet . . .

Killing was his trade. In his lifetime he had probably killed a hundred oryx. There had been nothing wrong with that. A hunter's work. But all of those had had splendid horns and shiny hides. While One-horn . . .

" . . . must die!" thundered the voice.

Morengáru bent his head. What difference would it make? One thing was as senseless as the next. This seemed to be the season for senseless things.

31

Every night since the "decision," Morengáru dreamed of One-horn. It may seem strange, but it was the same dream, and every time the old bull appeared the same way. He walked up slowly, stopped, and looked around hazily. First his forelegs folded, then his hind legs, and then, suddenly, his heavy head thumped against the ground with a resounding crash. Sometimes Morengáru woke up before it had got that far. But still he heard that heavy thud, so familiar had his dream become. It was an enigma, like everything to do with the oryx.

Where was One-horn heading? There was no explanation for such a straight line across the landscape. Unless the oryx was returning where he had started from. But if that was the case, everything became even more incomprehensible. Would the animal have covered all that distance for no other purpose than to look deep into Morengáru's eyes? He didn't even want to consider such a sinister possibility.

Hurrying more and more, he followed the trail. He covered long distances at speed. The oryx allowed himself time to graze, so Morengáru was gradually catching up with him. But day after day passed without even a glimpse of his quarry. Meanwhile he continued to wake with a start from the recurring oryx dream. Then he would sit and stare into the night for hours, his cold face turned toward the east. Somewhere there One-horn must be sleeping. Or was he awake? Could it be that he too lay staring into the dark? Did he too long for morning? Sometimes Morengáru thought he could feel the ground shaking under him and sat listening, aghast, until he realized it must be the oryx's head thudding heavily onto the ground once more. He pulled his cloak tight around himself and said aloud into the night, "Poor One-horn, you can't help it. You're bewitched."

It was obvious that an evil spirit must have taken possession of the oryx. That was the only explanation for One-horn's mysterious behavior. From the moment Morengáru had looked into his eyes and seen that malignant reflection of himself, everything had gone wrong. A *thahu* had fallen on Morengáru, and immediately fate had turned against him. That was why One-horn had to die. There could be no other reason. Why had he not realized this immediately! The old bull had to die. Not for his hide or his horn, not for his meat, but for his eyes, which held an image that should not exist. Only when those eyes closed forever would that gruesome specter disappear.

Just as lightning makes everything hidden in the dark night visible in a flash, so One-horn had come to show him something that would have been better left hidden.

32

Every morning, the landscape was fresh and young again; all colors appeared clean and new and dewy. But each morning, it was sad to see how that freshly born morning skin could not withstand the rough treatment of the wind and the sun. Before the day was half an hour old, the wind had dried out that tender skin. Then the sun would scorch it until it cracked and flaked off in innumerable tiny scales. Each morning, the earth here was flayed alive.

Morengáru left the open hill country behind and found himself in a wood that you might well call a forest of the dead. Ghostly bare trees and shrubs, bleached white, stripped bare of leaves and often even of branches. The wind whistled plaintively through those skeletons. Here, everything made you think of death and desolation. But One-horn's trail led on steadily, straight through this dismal wood.

On and on—into an even more fearsome wilderness. A jungle of man-high, dead-looking, thorny bushes, looming and fading behind swirling dust or dancing in blinding, shimmering air. And Morengáru followed, indifferent to heat and thirst.

And it was indifference, not courage, which made him outface two young lions who seemed determined to cut him off. Quite unexpectedly, he found himself eye to eye with them—totally unprepared—simply because he had stopped being vigilant. His bowstring was loose and his quiver covered.

When the two enormous beasts rose from the tall grass, growling, he realized they must be as surprised as he was. They were so close he could distinguish the flies on their still sleepy eyelids, and the pupils of their amber eyes, contracting against the sunlight. This would never have happened to him in the past. This is what happened to you if you went sleepwalking over the hills, blind to everything except the tracks of a ghostly animal. This is what you could expect if you let yourself be lured into the unknown and unreachable, every day another day's march beyond the horizon.

Morengáru was suddenly so conscious of his bitter loneliness, he did something preposterous. Instead of fleeing, or even tensioning his bow, he took a step forward and roared.

That is what happened. That was how he stood there, for one endless moment eye to eye with two ill-tempered lions. He roared with a true passion, his mouth wide open, head thrown back, tears streaming from his eyes. The lions were at least as amazed as he was. For a moment they stood looking at him, abashed, a bit overwhelmed. Then, opting for safety, they took off in long bounds.

Shaking from head to toe, Morengáru watched them. Then he smiled stupidly. And before long he was laughing loudly, until he could hear himself how false that laughter sounded. Ashamed, he clamped his mouth shut.

What had driven him to such a dare? A death wish? Contempt for death? He had no idea.

"Now, now, Morengáru, if the *morans* had seen that," he said aloud to himself. He sat down on the spot, because, suddenly, his legs couldn't carry his weight any longer.

"Did I really see that? Did I witness yet another heroic feat?" said a voice inside.

"You did see that, Masai. And I'd like to see you do the same!"

"Tell me, were you not in a trance this time? You were last time, weren't you—when you became *melombuki*, to your own stupid surprise?"

"You're just jealous."

"A pity all the same—that way a man can't even be proud of his own heroic actions."

"What would you know about it?"

"I was there."

"And me? I wasn't, I suppose."

"Not you. You were in a trance."

33

When had he started suffering from this talking sickness? It had crept up on him in one of those godforsaken camping spots, somewhere on the way. One day he must have started talking aloud for the first time, maybe just to hear somebody speaking. And it had become a habit. If only he could retrace his steps, back along the track that had long since been blown away with the dust. Go back to that one moment when he had started to think aloud, and undo that. It was an illness, a sign of decay. Walking, he constantly argued with himself, as if he were talking to someone else. What a strange impression he would make on other people! But there were no other people.

"Watch out, red ants!"

"Detour, thorny cactus."

"Hoof prints to the left of that hollow."

"Thorns."

"Tuft of fur."

"Blood."

Long before he actually saw the wounded lion, he picked up its bloody trail. A large lioness, dragging herself along flat on her belly. Bloody foam and slime everywhere. She must have a punctured stomach. She was dying; he heard her gurgling cough inside a clump of thorny bushes and made a respectful detour. Who could have done this but his One-horn? The mad one. The fearless one.

Probably the lioness had crept up on the solitary oryx as he was grazing—and he only noticed her at the last moment. If he had run away, the lioness would certainly have overtaken him, so the old bull had defended himself with his single deadly horn.

Morengáru went on, and the tracks already told him what he would find. Before the oryx had pulled himself free, the claws of the maddened lioness must have fatally wounded him. His tracks became more irregular, and more bloody. He had fallen repeatedly. Somewhere farther on, One-horn must be lying under the scrub, dying, or perhaps already dead. Morengáru approached slowly and carefully, his curiosity forcing him on.

From the grass under a thornbush a beautiful straight horn stuck out. There lay One-horn. As Morengáru approached, he tried once more to get up, but halfway he collapsed. For the last time his heavy head thumped down on the ground. Morengáru moved closer.

The dying oryx's eyes stared at him. The long lashes opened and closed more and more slowly. The light faded away in the curved mirrors, but they still caught something. Morengáru bent over, expecting to see himself reflected, like that time under the mimosa tree. But all he saw was the reflection of the empty sky, in which, slowly, a black dot appeared. It grew larger: a vulture, its wings spread wide.

No Morengáru distorted into a misshapen baboon, not even a Morengáru as he really was, a human being. Nothing but emptiness, and the circles drawn by death's messenger. What else had he expected?

34

One-horn was dead. It was all over. The path through the wilderness had come to an end. One-horn had ceased to exist. From here on, there would be no tracks to follow. All that was left was the wilderness. Morengáru sat down, shutting his eyes. After a while he let himself fall sideways, keeping the same posture. He lay there, folded double, like someone trying to make himself small.

The reality of time and space faded away around him. It felt as though he was sinking away into a twilight that became ever denser and darker. It couldn't end any other way. A herd animal simply couldn't exist by itself. What now? No more One-horn, no more tracks. Just day and night and endless space and time.

He heard vague sounds that gradually came closer, and opened his eyes. The sun no longer gave any warmth, and the trees on top of the hills caught the last of the light. Now he recognized the barking and the growling but even before that, he recognized the stench that preceded it: A large troop of baboons was approaching. Motionless, he waited.

The first ones he saw were the sentries, in strategic

positions ahead and to the side of the troop. Their task was to warn the others at the first sign of any danger. Already he could hear their warning *waaf*, a short, powerful sound, its meaning unmistakable. They had spotted him.

Morengáru did not feel entirely safe. Baboons were sometimes driven by dark urges and could attack quite unexpectedly. Killing one or two of the beasts in such circumstances was useless. The others would hurl themselves at you to avenge their mates. They could turn hysterical for no obvious reason and become so enraged that they lost all sense of danger.

He waited and watched how they changed places all together, as if on a signal. They took up attack positions. Females and young hung back a little, while the adult males made up a formidable vanguard. Morengáru could only do one thing: keep dead quiet and wait. If he stayed absolutely still, there was a good chance that they would ignore him after a while and move on.

A minute that lasted an eternity. A few barking sounds. Then the baboons dropped their threatening posture. The aggression that had united them evaporated. Now they showed interest in other things around them, and only the sentries kept a careful eye on him. Now, too, he could clearly distinguish the baboon king, even though all the large males were sitting in the same pose. That one male was bigger and more imposing as he sat there, his head raised watchfully, his bristly mane standing up. Even now, the slightest movement could be enough to arouse his mistrust and, with it, his fury.

For a long time Morengáru could see those malicious yellow eyes directed at him, and he knew it would be best to look away from time to time, so he would not create even the slightest hint of a challenge. What mean, ugly, obscene, dirty animals they were—those robbers of *shambas* and gardens! Noisy, stinking, constantly squabbling and fighting. Only that one large, gray male remained apart from all the commotion. Grim and dignified, he kept himself to one side. He was in every respect a splendid specimen, and he seemed to know it, the way he sat there smirking, with those long jaws full of impressive teeth. His hairless snout, with the big pouches, had an incredibly impudent expression.

Long after the troop of apes had disappeared over the hill, Morengáru kept seeing the provocative grin of the baboon king.

35

There was nothing left to live for. No trail to follow, no destination to look forward to. That night a large group of wild dogs came, drawn by the stench of the dead oryx. They stayed outside the glow of his fire, but he could hear them feeding and fighting. Early in the morning, the sky was full of the flapping of wings: vultures and crows, come to clean up the remains. In the first light of day, Morengáru sat watching the spectacle somberly. The vultures, cramming themselves, were a particularly dismal sight.

When the sun rose, he took his first good look at the plateau where he found himself. Acacias grew everywhere, their flat crowns full of white flowers. One tree towered above all the others. It was a baobab, a monkey bread tree. The legend that an angry god had pulled it out of the ground and planted it back upside down could have been true; the branches looked as if they hung upside down, as if they were actually roots. Lightning must have struck the colossal trunk. Morengáru imagined how it had happened: a ghostly white light, and then the scorching, all-consuming tongue of fire. The trunk was split down its whole length. In some spots, all you could see was a shiny black stripe, but in the middle, low above the ground, a gaping hole had been formed. There must have been water in it after the rainy season, and when that had finally evaporated, rot had set in. Now, with the rays of the sun shining into the hole, you could see the colorful fungi and the white, moldy wood. The baobab had been hollowed out, and the process continued day after day, with innumerable hordes of gnawing wood beetles, boring worms, rasping snails, veritable armies of vermin.

This time, he saw the baboons coming from a distance, in the same order as before. The young males darted around, ahead, and to the side, while the bossy older males walked in the center with the females and the young. But as soon as they spotted him, yesterday's performance was repeated. The barking grew louder and went up in pitch until it sounded like a constant, shrill, and fierce *waa-aa-aaf*. Only the males kept going and gathered together some thirty feet away from him. This time the king, alone, slowly came a few steps closer. Then he sat down. Motionless. He stared at Morengáru.

Morengáru stared back. He had an arrow ready in his bow, but something in the ape's attitude stopped him. The others sat down in a row behind their leader and stared relentlessly in his direction. Morengáru tried to understand what they intended. He concentrated mainly on the leader. It was clear that he was a real fighter; a champion, so outstanding that

111

there could be only one in each troop. Why was he sitting there so still? What did he want? As calmly as he could, Morengáru stared back, only too aware that his bow was completely useless against such a large troop of baboons. Without taking his eyes off the baboon king, he started moving back, slowly, a step at a time.

The leader stood up immediately and followed him at the same pace, step by step. And the row of males behind him did the same, quietly and silently.

Morengáru stopped. Instantly, the baboon king stopped too. And behind him, the whole troop stood rigid, close together.

Walking away was not a possibility. But what then? What was expected of him? What was the aim of this performance?

The king kept looking at him. His eyes were the amber color of his kind, but Morengáru thought he could see a strange red glow in them. This baboon's gaze was peculiarly compelling.

Another step back. And again, the king followed. Behind him, the whole rear guard rose to move forward a little. And then they all sat expectantly, watching him again.

Then the king made threatening gestures with his long fangs. He opened his mouth wide again and again, occasionally letting out a shrill, aggressive bark. His snout grew dark with anger. His mane stood up. Morengáru waited, absolutely still. After a time, the great baboon calmed down. He had been bluffing. Showing off. Playacting. He shook himself, turned his head away, fell back on all four legs, and walked off, throwing a last, surreptitious glance over his shoulder. And the whole troop followed him.

When the last ape had disappeared from view, Morengáru said aloud, "It is time to move on, Morengáru."

But the sun was high in the sky, and the afternoon passed, and Morengáru still sat in the same spot.

"In the east, there is nothing for me, and in the west there is nothing for me, in the north there is nothing for me, and in the south there is nothing for me. It is best to stay here."

36

When the baboons turned up again, the king started his threatening performance all over again. He shook his mane and ground his teeth. But this time, Morengáru did not wait for the rest of the show. He put the first arrow in his bow.

"How many arrows have you got, Kikuyu?"

"Nowhere near enough."

"So, you know what will happen."

He shook all the arrows out of his quiver and listened to the hoarse barking of the males who were gathering behind the leader. Then he drew his bow. He remembered the reflection of his face in the dark eyes of the oryx—how he had suddenly looked like a grinning baboon—and said grimly, "If that was the idea, just come and get me."

Morengáru, far from his fellow men and civilization, answered the challenge of the king in a baboon's voice: barking, baring his teeth. "Come on, then," he said.

The great ape didn't move immediately, but it wouldn't be long.

Morengáru noticed that the baboons had formed a semicircle, and sat there like spectators. They jumped up and down in their places, screeching and gesticulating. Only the king had not yet moved. His silver-gray mane stood out. He pulled up his black lips repeatedly, baring his long yellow teeth, but that was all.

Then it dawned on Morengáru: He was being challenged—not by the whole troop, but by the leader.

Morengáru the human being did not burst out laughing because he was being treated like a baboon. He did not fire his deadly arrows at the king, so the troop would be leaderless and thrown into confusion. Morengáru the human being allowed himself to accept this personal challenge, like a baboon. Bow, arrows, and spear he left behind. Slowly, erect, he walked toward the great baboon. Immediately, the baboon started moving too. He stood upright. His bent hind legs took long steps, while his long forelegs with the big claws dangled loosely by his side.

Was Morengáru out of his mind? He was strong and courageous, but that wouldn't be much use in a fight with an adult baboon. A huge male like that could twist an arm out of his body without any effort, and those yellow fangs were sharp as daggers. Perhaps he had been affected by his loneliness in the wilderness, by that futureless existence, and longed for a fast and violent end. Whatever the reason, he faced the baboon king, armed only with his knife.

Standing up to his full height, his broad chest puffed out, the great baboon suddenly stormed at him, grabbing with his lightning-fast arms. In his fury, the ape ignored the short, fierce knife thrusts that stabbed him below the ribs. Their force was nothing compared to the violence of the baboon's blows. He pulled at Morengáru's shoulders and arms, trying to get at his throat with his wide open jaws. But Morengáru moved his head this way and that to stay out of reach of those fangs. The other apes were screaming and jumping up and down like maniacs. Their barking and yelling was deafening, but not one of them tried to join the fight.

Morengáru was bleeding from several wounds. One of the grabbing claws had torn his face, and his shoulder had been ripped open by the snapping jaws. But the silver-gray mane itself was now bloodstained. The baboon kept trying a proven technique: He would grab at his opponent with all four claws, to throw him on his side and bite pieces out of him. He wanted to hold Morengáru by his head and tear his innards out with his hind legs, but Morengáru would not let him get a grip. Each time he managed to evade the claws and teeth, but he began to despair because his dagger thrusts seemed to have no effect on the baboon, and he could feel his strength ebbing.

In a fatal moment, the great ape saw an opening, and even though he wasn't moving half as fast as before, it was fast enough. Morengáru, weakened from blood loss, retreated too slowly and felt the incredibly strong claws destroy his collarbone. He screamed with pain and staggered back. Too late. The baboon king threw himself on him. He dug his teeth into Morengáru's right hip, and Morengáru felt the bite go through to the bone.

Everything around him disappeared into a red haze. The screaming and barking faded. He felt the heavy weight of the baboon king on top of him. Somewhere in his head he wondered why nothing else was happening. He couldn't know that his dagger thrusts had done their work. The baboon king was dead. Morengáru tried to get up, but his whole right side seemed to fail him. He did manage to push the dead baboon off, but he couldn't get up.

The baboons around him had fallen silent. In bursts, Morengáru could discern the animals watching him. What were they waiting for? Blood dripped into his eyes, and he shook his head. Hazily he stared from one to the other.

Nothing happened. After a while, he felt so weak he stopped trying to get up. He shut his eyes. Slowly, the pain eased. All sounds ceased. Somewhere, far away, a bird called again and again. He listened. Thoughts came to him, but they faded before he was really aware of them. It didn't matter anyway. Everything could stay the way it was.

Later, he screamed, but finally everything inside him became numb and still. By then he didn't think he'd ever feel the need to move again.

PART 4

the law of the tribe

37

Long before he opened his eyes, he became familiar with his surroundings through feel, taste, and smell—like a newborn child.

Every time he woke, his first sensation was pain; pain that spread through his whole body, and became gradually worse until he lost consciousness again. In between, with a vague feeling of surprise, he felt, tasted, smelled. His eyes were shut, at first because of dried blood, later out of habit. He lay in the position he had always slept: hands clamped around his knees, head pulled down between his shoulders. Around him, everything was steamy and clammy. Once, he noticed he was licking up moisture, without knowing where it came from. He didn't care. It was there. Then, for a while, it wasn't there, and he suffered thirst, but the thirst was part of the pain, the way the pain was part of the darkness.

He had no idea how long he had been hunched like that. Time had no meaning. Suddenly the stream of moisture on his cheek had come back, and he had drunk again. It came from somewhere above him, in a slow drip that flowed along his face and the rest of his body. The smell of decay and mold was everywhere around him, but that, too, was part of the darkness. He leaned against a soft, spongy wall that enclosed him and exuded a coolness that did his sore body good.

For a very long time—he had no idea exactly how long—there was no world for him apart from this black, all-encompassing dampness. The limits of this world were the spongy walls. He had no awareness of any world beyond that. Until, one time, the trickle of moisture increased, wetting his whole face. The crusts of blood that stuck his eyelids together slowly soaked off. The world became dusky, and then, little by little, lighter. Where before there had been only blackness, faint yellow and white colors now appeared.

It was the yellow and white of the fungi that covered the inside of the baobab tree. When he recognized them, his memory returned, and immediately he knew how he had come to be here. He had laboriously dragged his wounded, beaten body into this shelter. After the fight.

There had been a moment of consciousness when he seemed to look down on himself from a great height: a defenseless man surrounded by baboons. Next to him was the body of the baboon king. Indifferent, he had waited for the concerted attack that must surely follow, but nothing had happened. Once it started to get dark, the troop had withdrawn.

He remembered his amazement. They just left him behind with their defeated leader and went about their daily routine. They went to seek safety from the predators of the night in their usual sleeping tree. And he stayed behind, with no protection whatever. An enduring instinct for survival had made him look for cover. And the baobab, with its split trunk, had been close. He had managed to crawl to this narrow shelter, squeeze his tortured body into it, and collapse. Since then, there had been this cool darkness.

For a long time he had been shivering with fever, and the damp wall inside the tree trunk—where the sun hardly penetrated—had absorbed his heat, releasing healing moisture. He now understood that it must have been rain, or perhaps just the dew that collected in the tree above and seeped down along the branches and the trunk. The fungi and molds on the inside soaked it up and held it for a long time.

As he looked around, he discovered bunches of mushrooms everywhere and, just above his head, a couple of enormous flat fungi on which puddles had formed. Whenever those natural bowls overflowed, the water trickled down his cheek. All he had to do to drink was stick out his head. For the moment, that was what he needed most.

There were times when his whole body seemed to be on fire. Then he searched for fresh spots of dampness to press against. At other times he sank into a sort of unconsciousness. Insects swarmed around his wounds. He shook and shivered in his dreams and was woken by thirst. Then he would lick up some rainwater, stare around in a daze, and sink away again.

He guessed that he must have been in the hollow baobab for days. Occasionally a few rays of sunlight came in through the opening. Then everything around him, the moldy wood, the fungi and mushrooms, would take on a golden glow. At night he could see stars, or clouds moving across the moon. The opening above his head was like a high window. Sometimes he heard indistinct sounds—mostly birds and occasionally the *waaf* of a baboon—but the world outside didn't interest him.

Morengáru knew how to endure pain. He moved as little as possible. Slowly the fever eased, and his head cleared. And with that returning clarity, hunger began to trouble him.

The baobab provided everything. Caterpillars, bugs, beetles, and larvae lived in the rotting wood. Morengáru ate them all. With one hand he picked up every ant, every ladybug, every worm that came his way on the fungi and popped it into his mouth. He had discovered that he couldn't use his other hand. The time came when he was strong enough to crush the shell of a snail between his fingers: more good protein. Not long after that, he caught his first lizard.

Now that finding food was becoming essential, he began to wonder what had happened to his spear, bow, and arrows. For the first time, he tried to climb out of the hollow baobab. It was only then he discovered that his right leg refused to cooperate. That threw him into a panic. What had happened to him? He struggled to get up, but every time he had to give up and resign himself to waiting.

Once he heard a scuffling close by, outside the trunk. He lifted his head, and saw the face of a baboon in the opening. The beast peered in, grimaced, and smacked his pink lips, making a chirping sound. There was nothing threatening in his attitude, only curiosity. Morengáru looked back at him, without feeling any fear. He had gone beyond that. What could happen to him that hadn't happened before?

After a while, the baboon's head disappeared. The sound receded. And Morengáru slowly dozed off.

38

After that, a baboon regularly came to have a look. And only after many visits did Morengáru realize it was always the same one. A young male with a twisted ear. Sometimes his cheek pouches were still full of food, sticking out on both sides of his snout like balls. His fur was rough, but the bare skin of his snout was a rosy gray. That, and his clear brown eyes with soft purple lids, made him look a bit like a surprised human.

Folded inside his hiding place, Morengáru wondered why the others never came to look, while this one came so regularly. He often heard the troop go by, quarreling and barking, always preceded by that stench. He also wondered how the animals would react once he reappeared.

His longing for sun and space became stronger. One day, as soon as the sun was up, he started a determined effort to get out of his hiding place, which was fast becoming like a prison. Pulling with one arm, pushing with one leg, he struggled toward the opening, sliding back again and again on the slippery molds and mushrooms. Then, after wriggling and gasping in the dark, he rolled into the world, blinking in the bright sunlight. He landed panting in the grass at the foot of the tree. There he lay, while the slime from the fungi dried to a white powder on his skin. For the first time he could have a look at himself from top to toe. His panting stopped, and he held his breath in horror. What the protecting darkness had hidden all this time was now mercilessly revealed by the light: his shriveled right arm and his knotty, bent right leg. The wounds had healed, the skin had closed over the torn ligaments and muscles, but where the bones had been broken, he now saw strange growths, and the knee joint wouldn't work.

He looked at himself and cried.

39

All day long, Morengáru was busy eating the fruits of the baobab. They lay everywhere around the huge trunk. It took a lot of skill to break open their hard, tough skins, but he finally worked out the best way: He could crack them open by hitting them against a rock. The white kernel had no taste, but was very nourishing. For the first time in ages, his stomach felt satisfied.

The thought of eating the dried-out fruits of the baobab had only occurred to him when he saw the baboons doing it. They were real omnivores. Flowers, seeds, tubers, and pips, as well as ants, beetles, and locusts, were their daily fare. Scorpions were popular too, but he wasn't yet game to try them; his single hand wasn't nearly fast enough. The baboons had no trouble with that. It was amazing how smartly they could grab one and bite it in half before the poisonous tail could get to them.

Many of the seeds and pips the baboons collected proved inedible, or were only digestible after being soaked in water for a day. The baboons had a more convenient method for that; they kept those pips in their cheek pouches until the saliva had softened them enough to be chewable.

He had been surprised how nimble-fingered these animals were. For quadrupeds, they had very finely formed hands. It took a while to become aware of this, but a baboon could use the same claw he used for all his heavy climbing and digging to work a grain of sand out of his own eye. Because they walked mostly on the calluses below their wrists, they had kept the sensitivity in their fingers. Baboons' hands were very like human hands.

When the red sun set the western plain on fire, the stench

and the racket told him the baboon troop was approaching. He waited, unafraid, for he knew by now they would leave him alone. They had long since stopped taking up attack positions when they saw him sitting under the baobab, and accepted his presence. Unconcerned, they went about their business as if he had never been an enemy, except that every now and then a large male would come and pay his respects.

At first, Morengáru had found this worrying, because he felt quite defenseless. A colossal beast like that could easily tear him to pieces, but this never seemed to occur to the animal. Like the one with the twisted ear, he usually came just to look. Sometimes he performed what looked like a greeting. Morengáru had learned to tell the difference between a baboon who was relaxed and one who felt uneasy.

If a baboon was scared, he sat up rigidly, or walked with knees and elbows bent, ready to jump away any time. If he was at ease, he sat casually, his wrists resting loosely on his knees, or walked with a smooth, easy gait. You had to watch the tail, too. A tail that stood up, stiff, indicated fear. Once you knew things like that, you could take them into account. But you also needed to know that a tail standing up stiff could just as well mean that the grass was damp with dew, and baboons don't like dampness. Such a mistake could be dangerous. On one occasion, not reading the signals had nearly been fatal.

One of the tallest males seemed scared, but turned out to be looking for a fight. The animal suddenly threw up his head and uttered a series of *kek-kek-kek* noises, faster and faster until it became a scream. Morengáru was so surprised he sat where he was. The females and young nearby, who knew better, made themselves scarce. The male started beating the ground to left and right and suddenly stormed at

Morengáru, who hadn't moved—he couldn't even think of running for it—and that turned out to be the correct thing to do. Right in front of him, the baboon stopped dead, growled a bit, and then calmly sat down. It had been a bluff. To be on the safe side, Morengáru had carefully kept his teeth covered. Smiling at a baboon was about the most foolish thing you could do. And since that occasion, he knew how to deal with such a fit of fury.

During the hour between sunset and night, before the troop withdrew to the big mimosa that was their sleeping tree, the baboons seemed very sociable. The adults sat grooming each other, picking fleas out of each other's fur, the tireless young romping around them. The near-adult ones also became playful, chasing each other around, like a game of tag. Occasionally their high spirits turned destructive, and they would furiously attack a bush, ripping it up as if it were their common enemy. Their anger was obviously put on, but as they ripped off leaves and branches they spun out of control. And then, just as suddenly, they calmed down.

There was a loud *waaf*, and the whole troop obediently started moving to the safety of the branches of their sleeping tree. With a sigh, Morengáru watched them disappear. Soon he would crawl back into the baobab, his own sleeping tree.

He vaguely recalled the story an old *mundumugu* had told about the origin of the baboon. In primeval times, man's ancestor had had a backward brother whom he chased away and who, in the wilderness, had become worse and worse. That was the baboon.

40

Now that Morengáru could walk again, more or less, he gradually ventured farther from the baobab. He would never run again the way he used to. Nearly a whole season had passed since the fight, and it was hard locating the spot where his fatal clash with the baboon king had taken place. His skeleton was nowhere to be found, nor was Morengáru's spear. He found some remnants of his quiver, half eaten by a jackal. He didn't even bother looking for the arrows; the tips would have long since been ruined by rust. But he hoped he would find his spear, or else his knife.

For days he searched, step by step. Nothing. Had the baboons dragged the spear away? He had observed that they paid close attention to any strange object, often picking it up and carrying it around for a while. Stubbornly he kept looking, and even when he had really given up hope, he kept his eyes open for any clues. Meanwhile, it usually was a full day's work finding enough to eat.

Now that he had to live on his hands and feet a lot of the time, he got to know the tiny field animals he used to overlook: the creatures that scratched around diligently under the dead leaves—shrews, field mice, wood mice, rats, all sorts of rodents—each with their own maze of little tunnels through the tall grass.

He set traps made of twisted grass stalks, and kept catching the same kind of field mouse: a small, scruffy, rust-brown animal with an orange belly. Its bright black little eyes looked fearless and curious, even at the very last moment before the hand that caught it squeezed the life out of it. Other kinds proved to be less adventurous or careless, and didn't let themselves be caught: like the larger field mouse with the gray-brown back and yellow-white belly, or the sandy-colored one with the black stripe on its back, and, unfortunately, the largest of all those rodents, the gray rat with the big, round eyes.

He regularly crossed paths with the baboons. At first he had to stop himself scrabbling head over heels back to the baobab. Ridiculous, of course. As if they couldn't find him there if they wanted him. But they didn't treat him as an enemy at all; rather as an equal, one of their own kind.

He had to get used to this uncertain existence among these alien "friends." He had no choice. He lived on their territory. He had to make himself overcome his horror and disgust, and adapt as best he could. That was his only chance of survival. He was the clumsiest four-footer for miles around, and he was at the mercy of the animals. For his own safety, it was best to stay close to the baboons.

Baboons would not easily be surprised by any beast of prey. They had the habit of frequently stopping whatever they were doing and rapidly looking all around. Their sight may not have been much sharper than Morengáru's, but a predator had to deal with some fifty pairs of eyes and didn't have much chance of staying unnoticed for long. And no matter how frightened a baboon might be, how fast he might try to flee, he would always alert the others first with his warning bark.

But it was not only for their watchfulness that Morengáru sought out the baboons whenever he could; they actually afforded him real protection. Often they showed remarkably little fear, and would quietly continue what they were doing after spotting a predator. It was clear that, together, they felt strong enough to take on a great cat or a wild pig. Only in an extreme case would they take off. If that happened,

Morengáru was in a desperate situation. Baboons could run very fast, and at a pinch climb up a tree, but it was different for him. Even a wild dog or a hyena could easily beat him, and he no longer had the speed to get out of the way. Fortunately, the baboons' threatening display usually worked.

The only animal they really respected was the lion. Luckily the lion that turned up one day recognized the slow straggler as one of the dreaded humans. While it paused, openmouthed with surprise, Morengáru managed to catch up with his retreating protectors, unharmed.

Once high in a tree, the baboons felt safely out of reach of their enemies. They could sleep comfortably on quite thin branches. Morengáru always went off to his baobab at nightfall. He climbed into the narrow space, blocking the opening with a few stout branches so he would not be surprised in his sleep. Only the young baboons were still curious about this different behavior. The others had by now accepted it as just one of his many peculiarities.

41

He still had a lot to learn. More than once, he had the uncomfortable feeling that he had only just escaped being attacked by one of those big males, without having any idea what he might have done to arouse his fury.

Learning how to be threatening was perhaps the most important thing. There was a lot involved. It required self-control, and you needed to know exactly how far you could go. Raising your eyebrows was the mildest form. Sometimes you needed to repeat this, sticking your head forward emphatically. If that didn't work, it was time for some irritated hand movements, like lightly hitting the ground, or the air. Getting up growling, while stamping your feet, was a pretty serious threat, particularly if you looked the other straight in the eye. It became even more serious if you opened your mouth wide at the same time, drawing your lips well back—even though your teeth were pretty insignificant for a baboon. Grinding your teeth showed you really meant business. And if even that didn't work, you were in a dangerous position, because it meant the other wanted to see if you were bluffing or not. Fortunately things never got that far for Morengáru.

Meanwhile, it had become clear to him that baboons had a kind of language. By using certain gestures and expressions, they could get each other to understand all sorts of things. A loud, barking *arr-ah* meant a greeting, he knew for certain, while a vicious *kek-kek-kek* implied a refusal or a threat. A long-drawn-out and repeated *arr-ah* was a warning, particularly if it came from the sentries. This instantly made them take up fighting positions. Closing ranks, moving forward, or retreating, all had their fixed sounds.

Aaay-eh, the young called when they were hungry, and *la-la-la* while frolicking, for baboons giggle as often and for the same reasons as people. *Unh-unh-unh*, a baboon would groan in pure pleasure while being groomed. And if you heard a trilling, long *oah-oah-oah* you could be sure one of them would be shaking his head, beside himself with delight.

Tsjilp-tsjilp-tsjilp was usually a sign of curiosity or a request to be allowed to join in a game. Screaming and yelling the baboons did in all sorts of tones, high and low. The shrieking of an adult carried at least as far as the roar of a lion. If the whole troop got going, the din was so deafening Morengáru had to cover his ears.

But the most mysterious sound of all was the *oohrrrng* that sometimes sounded when two or three of the males sat together. He could never discover what the meaning of that might be.

42

It wasn't surprising that the baboons were so aggressive. They had to be. They lived mostly on the ground, often on open, treeless plains. How else could they be, with leopards, hyenas, and wild dogs all around them, and so few ways of escape? And it was no more surprising that such pugnacious animals would fly at each other at the slightest thing. The near-adult males were the worst, and their fights could sometimes cause sudden agitation. They threatened the safety of the whole group by disturbing the order required to act swiftly and unanimously. The troop had to be able to move like a well-drilled army, whether in attack or flight.

It was necessary to maintain strict discipline, and this was taken care of by the same males who acted as sentries and who formed the vanguard when danger threatened. If there was a fight going on anywhere, one of them would come running to put an end to it. Only rarely did this lead to actual physical punishment—that whole code of threats wasn't there for nothing. The dangerous fangs only went into action if all else failed.

Morengáru couldn't see himself controlling those young rebels by bluffing. He could imagine only too well how one of the brutes would hurl himself at him, biting and clawing. And yet he had to maintain his position in the troop somehow.

By now it had become clear to him that he ranked at the top because he had killed the baboon king. But why none of the males had challenged his position was a mystery to him. He worried about it in the solitude of his sleeping tree, afraid of doing anything that might be taken for a sign of weakness.

You could see what position a baboon had in the troop by the space the others allowed him. Morengáru had discovered he could go and sit down wherever he liked, and every baboon immediately got up for him when he approached. Even the dominant males made conciliatory gestures before they ventured close to him. With much smacking of lips, they indicated they had no bad intentions.

Morengáru tried to maintain a scowl, hoping his "subjects" would wisely stay out of his way. He wanted to gain time to study their behavior and learn the meaning of all their gestures, grimaces, and sounds. Perhaps that way he would be able to work out how a baboon king was expected to behave.

As a hunter, Morengáru was familiar with many codes of behavior in the animal world. He knew, for instance, how an antelope made it clear that he was the boss of the herd. He knew the exhausting display of power of the bull rhinoceros, who, snorting and stamping, marked out his territory. And he had almost died laughing, watching a zebra stallion who kept trying hopelessly to shit a larger heap than his rival. That's the way zebras are. But he had never hunted baboons, and so knew next to nothing about their habits.

Being king of the baboons, Morengáru had discovered

that all he had to do was to glare at a troublemaker with big, angry eyes. He felt ridiculous, but fortunately the villains didn't think so. The occasional time this stern look proved inadequate, all he had to do was sit up straight and show his teeth. In an extreme case he was forced to take a few steps forward and hit the ground threateningly with his good arm. During the past few days he had gone as far as imitating the mean barking.

Roars like a lion, barks like a baboon, and the rest of the time talks to himself like a senile old man. Behold Morengáru, he thought to himself.

43

He was learning fast. He got used to the sight of baboons who turned their buttocks toward him as a sign of submission whenever he approached, looking at him over their shoulders with a humble look in their yellow eyes. Sometimes he had trouble keeping a straight face, particularly if it was one of the champions. It was too stupid, if you thought about it. Here he was, a king surrounded by subjects who were better at everything than he was. They were better at climbing, running, and fighting, but it simply never occurred to them, and so they rarely challenged him.

Little by little, he worked out how he could limit the exhausting display of strength that fitted his position to a minimum of voice, gesture, and attitude. He also learned the correct way of behaving toward the champions, who apparently had the right to come and sniff around him regularly, and even touch him occasionally. On their part, they were supposed to first make submissive, or at least reassuring gestures, but on his part he was supposed to submit to these approaches without moving. Fortunately, the champions were not as keen on such intimate contact as the others in the troop, and it was up to him, as holder of the highest rank, to decide how often he welcomed such greetings. Usually a disapproving look or a raised eyebrow was enough to keep away a male who got too friendly.

Though there were a lot of fights, the champions rarely fought among themselves. That was understandable, for if it ever came to a test of strength, it was a formidable business. If two of them didn't get on, they wisely stayed out of each other's way. Only if one tried to push another from his place in the rank would it turn into a fight. But for the moment it seemed that every ape was content with his own place, and daily life was relatively peaceful.

It was the young who made for unity in the troop. Without exception, the adult animals loved the playful little ones. Even the grimmest male behaved tolerantly toward them, and often treated them with surprising gentleness. If one of these ill-natured beasts settled down comfortably and made it clear that he was in a good mood for a change, the young would immediately be attracted. They would deliberately play closer and closer and try in all sorts of ways to get him involved in their games. Sometimes they managed, and you could see a big male clumsily joining in the fun. The first time Morengáru observed it, he couldn't believe his eyes. This giant even let them clamber all over him.

One old ape in particular, with a completely gray face, appeared to tolerate the young to a remarkable extent. And sometimes you would swear he was doing it with a purpose. The way he dealt with them made it seem clear he was involved in their upbringing. More than once he let himself be attacked by a crowd of excited young ones, pretending to desperately defend himself, but all the time quietly teaching them the techniques of attack and defense. When he started getting bored with the game, he would play dead for a bit, and the young ones would play on by themselves.

Gray, as Morengáru started calling him, was exceptional in many ways. Despite his crumbling, rotting teeth, he was part of the top group. If he had to assert his power, he had precious little to threaten with—even his fangs were worn down—and yet his authority was never challenged. Strange.

Grinning to himself, Morengáru had to admit that the perpetual trials of strength among the half-grown males seemed only too familiar. A baboon who wanted to get to the top needed the same qualities required for a top rank among the Masai. He had to fight constantly for the next step up. In the course of his life he worked himself higher and higher up by eliminating one rival after another. Strength and courage were the first requirements; sheer physical strength and fighting spirit were decisive.

And yet there had to be more to it than that. Wasn't Gray himself living proof that muscles and fangs weren't the only equipment in the fight for rank? It was quite possible he had worked his way up in the usual way, with guts and violence, but then how could he now stay at the top? This riddle made Morengáru more and more curious about him, and he started observing Gray closely. It was amazing how calm and confident the old ape's behavior always was; you would almost say dignified. Seeing him going about his business, it was hard to imagine him ever doing anything noisy or frantic.

Eventually Morengáru discovered that Gray's self-confidence rested to a large extent on the safe knowledge that his back was covered by his allies. The veteran must have made some sort of pact with two slightly younger males, both champions. If one of these three had a problem, the others immediately came to his aid. And no adversary was equal to their joint action.

The three were so powerful that they had long since taken over the actual leadership of the troop—perhaps not openly, but in an indirect and quite natural way. Yet they continued to treat the "king" with all due respect, a contradiction that amazed Morengáru. But their puzzling behavior reassured him that he could, at least for the time being, feel safe.

The situation may have suited the three allies. Perhaps, being seasoned veterans, they could foresee that without someone above them—even if only a figurehead—there would inevitably be a fatal power struggle among them. It was all confusing and inexplicable, but as long as the three were satisfied with the setup, he wouldn't be so dumb as to want to know better!

44

When he walked among the baboons, Morengáru did his best to appear self-assured. It wasn't always easy, for he couldn't get used to the idea that his life depended on being able to pretend. It was all show, and he didn't feel comfortable with that. He felt ridiculous standing there threatening with a mouth full of human teeth, but time and again the performance seemed to work, and he gradually gained confidence.

Glaring furiously at rebellious young males, he tried to convey the controlled savagery that, he assumed, should mark this baboon-of-baboons. And meanwhile he often had to stop himself lowering his eyes when facing their sultry, murderous looks. Hindered by his half-lame leg and his uselessly dangling arm, he sometimes found it hard to swagger past one of those dreaded fighters with the right degree of carelessness.

When he felt uncertain, he had a sneaking suspicion that the three real leaders of the troop were having him on, that they were playing a game with him. It was their submissive behavior that seemed so suspicious to him then—the way they turned their terrifying snouts away from him, all the while leering at him with their unreadable eyes. And the way they tried, almost comically, to make their big, rough, muscular bodies as small as possible when he approached. . . .

He feared that one day they would get fed up with it all, and there would be a sudden end to their pretense. Then they would unanimously rise for him, but instead of standing aside they would surround him and tear him apart—while he, the "king," would have done his best to the very last moment to perform his role as authentically as possible. . . .

But this was his imagination running wild. If they wanted to kill him, they would do so straight out. Animals didn't behave in such complicated ways. Although, you had to admit, it would be a fiendish joke. But since when did animals have a sense of humor? Reasoning with himself like this, Morengáru managed to control his panic. He must not burden these simple baboons with human guile. Better to trust what he could see, and not look for hidden intentions behind their actions.

Gradually he began to trust Gray, whom he never saw pestering a lesser ape, or abusing his position of power. He couldn't suspect this patriarch of a mean cat-and-mouse game; that wouldn't be at all like him. He wasn't only fearless, but truly kind.

For instance, Gray had taken pity on the young male with the deformed ear, the one who had first shown an interest in Morengáru. He was obviously in a bad state, undernourished, and with festering sores round his eyes and mouth. Some kind of disease had attacked the skin on his head so badly that his skull was almost bare.

Such a sick baboon, barely able to keep up with the troop, was a pitiable sight. It was not surprising that he was afraid of getting behind, because even a wild dog or a jackal would have no trouble finishing him off. Gray took him under his care, letting him walk next to him in the middle of the group, and even letting him sleep next to him. That way, the young animal had a chance. Gray took this role very seriously. Sometimes he turned over heavy rocks for his weaker mate, and sat watching him grab the ants and beetles that had gathered in the damp darkness.

To Morengáru's surprise, the young baboon's sores started healing, and even the skin disease diminished slowly, although, even when he was eventually strong enough to romp around with the other young males, he had an ugly bald patch on his skull. So Morengáru secretly called him Baldy. He often had to laugh at him, for, having such a mighty protector, he became a bit of a loudmouth. If one of the others threatened Baldy, he would run screeching to Gray, sit down close to him, and glare at his opponent with eyebrows raised high.

Gray kept a suitable distance from Morengáru. It wouldn't occur to him to try to get close, the way Baldy often did. Baldy constantly tried to groom Morengáru, without ever taking offense at being rebuffed.

Grooming was not only a way of keeping each other's fur clean, it was also a way of showing submission or friendship. The animals obviously enjoyed being groomed, as they always sat or lay in an attitude of blissful relaxation. The females groomed the most. Animals of equal rank groomed each other, but animals of low rank were also expected to groom the bossy males. And the higher the rank, the less you groomed.

Morengáru often wondered if Gray was aware that he, and not the "baboon king," actually led the troop. Not only did he manage to maintain discipline in his own restrained way, but decisions were up to him. Morengáru felt like a kind of retired king, not really burdened with responsibility.

The troop seemed to adjust easily to this curious state of affairs. Morengáru wasn't expected to have much to do with his "subjects." Apart from occasionally putting up with being groomed, he usually managed to keep a certain distance. When it was a matter of fight or flight, they didn't wait for his example. Instead they looked to Gray and his allies to see what to do. Gradually, a situation developed where you could really talk of two leaders. But as Morengáru and Gray were on good terms, this did not cause a power struggle, and the troop seemed to have no problem with it.

Calmly, without behaving as if he was the king himself, Gray took on all the tasks Morengáru, voluntarily or otherwise, gave up. Gray appeared comfortable as the bearer of the king's orders and the maintainer of his unassailable power. For Morengáru, this wasn't such a bad state of affairs. He felt more and more secure, and ventured farther and farther afield with the troop. And that was vital, for food around the baobab was becoming scarce.

45

On the open plain, Morengáru occasionally got into trouble because he was so slow. The baboons were amazingly fast compared to him. Normally, this caused no problems, because the troop moved from one feeding place to the next at a slow trot, in close formation. Anyone who moved too far ahead was mercilessly dealt with by Gray. But there were situations when the whole mob took off helter-skelter at a warning *aar-ah* from a sentry. Then Morengáru had to get away as best he could, which made him feel terribly vulnerable, because usually he had no idea what the danger was. But up to now he had been lucky.

Once, in the dry grass, he happened on an enormous python, the apes' most deadly enemy. The gigantic constrictor couldn't get enough leverage for its tail on the flat ground and was slowed by the tough grass stalks. It lunged at Morengáru, but missed. Before it could try again, Morengáru hit it with a large stone, breaking its backbone. In his terror, he kept smashing the stone into the long, twisting body until, half-paralyzed and powerless, it was easy prey for the returning troop of excited baboons. Morengáru was lucky to salvage a small piece for himself.

He had always known baboons liked meat. When a baboon troop raided a Kikuyu settlement, they didn't just strip the gardens, but dogs would disappear, too. And yet he was almost shocked to see how, once they got over their fear, they ripped the dead snake open with teeth and claws and devoured it like real carnivores. Morengáru himself moved apart with the liver, which he gobbled up, raw and bloody, his eyes shut tight with pleasure. What a change from seeds and roots or a morsel of field mouse!

The beast in him had been awakened, and the beast craved meat—raw, red, bloody meat. It was as if his teeth were getting sharper; he wanted to use them more to threaten angrily, like the others. When he was like that, his face almost felt like a snout. Growling and eating greedily and then having a good sleep in the shade—that was often all he wanted to do. This part of him felt more at home in the wilderness, and became more and more dominant. He could almost feel himself turning into a baboon, his fingers good for climbing, his lips drawn back, teeth bare, mouth wide, ready to bite and tear, but also to go *kek-kek-kek* and to groom. Of course, this came from spending so much time in the wilderness, but perhaps the beast had always been in him, somewhere under his ribs, under his skull. It was part of him.

He often thought about this. Despite all the *mundumugus*, the beast had not let go of people. It had come with them out of the wilderness and waited patiently for them to return there.

46

Living with baboons had its advantages. Never before had he had such calm, uncomplicated companions. They didn't complain if conditions went against them, they weren't afraid of ghosts and spirits and knew no *thahus*, and didn't go on about duties and standards.

Like every animal in the wilderness, Morengáru gradually became one with nature around him. One with the hills, the wind, and the undulating grass. This was his world, his sun, his dew—and for him there was no other. Once he was used to the stillness of the plain, all sounds and colors acquired their own eloquent meanings.

And yet . . . he still suffered the "talking sickness" from time to time, even if the words were gradually losing their meanings. He'd said everything he could think of saying so often before that he frequently broke off in mid-sentence, starting the next one without even stopping for breath. He no longer expressed his moods through what he said, but through how he said it—a monotonous mumbling of half sentences. It reached the stage where he just uttered sounds, puzzling him when he heard himself.

"There's. That's. Back. Don't lose." It had nothing to do with real talk anymore. It was more like an uninterrupted singsong nobody listened to, not even Morengáru himself. And there was something else. The more he got used to the baboons' company, the more he learned their language. *Kek-kek-kek*, he would say, shaking his head at a plant he knew was poisonous. And *eehk-eehk-eehk*, quietly, seeing a scorpion, and *oon-oon* when, to his delight, he found a plump root or an edible worm.

Sometimes Gray would look up surprised when Morengáru

made a human sound, for they had got used to moving through the plain together. Seeing Gray's formidable figure always reassured Morengáru, particularly if the wind made his magnificent mane stand out, so that he looked even more solid. Seeing Gray's surprise, Morengáru resolved to mind his language.

47

Half asleep in the moonlit night, Morengáru heard sounds that seemed to call him. It must be the whining of the wild dogs gathered round a prey that was too large for them. They called to each other over great distances, as if one pack called to another for help. Morengáru mumbled softly, "You here. Good. Sleep."

Stars fell from the sky, and clumps of tangled grass rolled over the plain like runaway ghosts, ahead of the wind. The dogs kept whining to each other. Somewhere among the packs must be their terrified prey. Nothing to be done about it. Its time had come. The time would come for everything and everyone. You had no say in it. There might not be much sense in living on, but as long as your time hadn't come, you had to. That's how it was.

"Sleep, Morengáru, king of the baboons, and dream."

But sleep wouldn't come. The whining of the wild dogs sounded higher, more excited, in shorter bursts, as if they were straining to catch up with something. Probably an old or wounded antelope who had dropped behind the herd. They could smell anything old and weak!

Morengáru rolled himself into a ball, knees to his chin, and tried to sleep. The scent of his own body and of the fungi and molds was all around him, familiar and reassuring. Here, in the baobab, it stayed comfortable for a long time, while the cold night wind blew outside.

"Sleep, Morengáru, and dream your faraway dreams. Dream of gardens and dancing. Dream of the big drum."

In a while, he would go down to Kimani's *shamba*. Kariuki and Kupanya would be there, too. He would stretch out comfortably by the fire and listen to their stories. Sometimes Kariuki played his melancholy music across Kimani's mad monologues. And Kupanya bent toward him, smiling, whispering something about a magic herb.

Morengáru scratched himself in his sleep and stopped worrying about the whining of the wild dogs—but it seemed to take an awfully long time to get to Kimani's place. . . .

He woke up with a start and sat up. Moonlight shone through the opening, white but sinister. He peered outside. The crown of the sleeping tree looked blue in that light. The sleeping apes were like the ghosts of monsters. It was all unearthly, nightmarish. He didn't want to look anymore, so he rolled himself into the smallest possible ball.

Just before he fell asleep again, he realized that the whining of the wild dogs had stopped. So they had finally got their prey. For the rest of that night, he had no more dreams.

PART 5

the voice of the king

48

Morengáru sat in the shade of the baobab, patiently rubbing
the end of a thick branch against a stone. It was the hottest
part of the afternoon. Around him, the baboons sat grooming
each other, or just listening, like every afternoon at this time.
They were drowsy and sluggish, and showed barely any
interest in what he was doing. He intended to make a weapon
somewhere between a short spear and a club.

While he was working, he heard a sharp cry that he
recognized as the alarm cry of a dik-dik, a dwarf antelope. He
looked up into the blinding sunlight. Gray had discovered an
acacia tree covered in seedpods a bit farther along and was
contentedly munching them. In his panic to make sure he
got his share, Baldy had jumped slap-bang into the shrub
under the acacia, where the dik-dik must have been hiding.
The terrified little animal took off, zigzagging over the field
like a hare, and immediately the whole troop of baboons
stormed after it.

Morengáru stared after them. They weren't likely to catch
the dik-dik, who could run just as fast and was on its home
ground too, knowing every escape route. Morengáru was
already turning his attention back to his work when something
quite ridiculous happened.

The joke was at the expense of one of the largest males,
the one he had started calling Shifty-eyes, because of his

inflamed tear glands. Lying apart from the others, he looked sleepy, dopey, and at first glance quite innocent. But Morengáru knew better. Shifty-eyes had a habit of suddenly grabbing any young one who was careless enough to come within his reach and, with much unnecessary display of strength, forcing him into submission. Morengáru had been watching Shifty-eyes lately. There was something treacherous in that huge animal's demeanor. The way he usually sat—eyes shut, hands passively in his lap—made you think of a mantis assuming a praying position while waiting for an insect to be taken in by its harmless looks. He had noticed that Gray had to intervene regularly when Shifty-eyes pushed a squealing young one roughly down onto the ground, or bit one rather too hard on the neck in what was supposed to be a game. It was not surprising that this bad-tempered ape was often on his own.

The escaping dik-dik hadn't noticed the drowsing baboon, and headed his way. Shifty-eyes, alerted by the noise of the others, slowly opened his inflamed eyes and saw the dik-dik coming toward him. With a mighty yell he shot up, but the dik-dik reacted faster. It saw its way barred, mid-leap, and in a panic kicked out its thin, strong legs—four hard hooves, each split into two sharp points—and landed fair and square on that hairy, surprised giant.

It was as if the formidable chest of the amazed baboon bounced the little dik-dik into its next leap. How else could the tiny antelope stand on top of Shifty-eyes one moment, and be four leaps away the next? It kept running for its life, the whole madly excited troop of baboons in hot pursuit, with Shifty-eyes in the lead.

Morengáru exchanged a glance with Gray, who had stayed quietly in the acacia tree. Just like him not to take any notice of the commotion. He wasn't silly enough to give up his great spot for a useless chase. But he wasn't picking any more pods. Instead, he bent forward on his branch, peering straight down. His snout was hidden by his raised gray mane as he sat with bent neck, looking down tensely. What could he see there?

For a moment, Morengáru's attention was diverted by the racket of the hunting mob. The dik-dik had reached the edge of the plain and was clambering up a rocky hill. Even from that distance you could hear the clicking of its hooves on the bare rock. Shifty-eyes was closest to it now—showing again how easily you could misjudge that odd animal. Only moments ago he was dozing in the shade, but now he was shrieking, his mouth wide open, his mane standing up, and his tail stretched out.

In contrast with the frenzied behavior of the baboon behind it, the dik-dik was in control of its movements, even while running for its life. It made daring but calculated leaps, each time landing elegantly on its trembling legs and instantly taking off again, its body flashing red-brown in the sunlight. And all the time it sounded the alarm cry that gave it its name, and made it hated by all hunters because it warned all the animals far and wide. Morengáru had always considered the dik-dik to be a plague, but now he could see the tiny antelope in a different light.

Fighting an opponent his own size wasn't for Shifty-eyes, but apparently this defenseless little creature had raised his mighty fury. So eager was he for blood that he charged up the hill like a mad thing, without tactics or plan, wildly crashing into rocks.

It was alarming to watch this ferocious baboon chasing a creature no larger than a hare, which he obviously wanted to rip to pieces. After a whole morning's eating, Shifty-eyes' behavior couldn't possibly be due to hunger, nor was the dik-dik a threat to the young. It must be pure bloodthirstiness. Morengáru decided he would keep an even more careful eye on this unpredictable character.

He looked back to Gray, who was still peering down from his branch. There must be something in the bushes under that tree. Morengáru was curious, but he was distracted by the click-clack of the little split hooves on the sloping rocks and the obstinate *dik-dik-dik*. Shifty-eyes had now stormed far ahead of the others, a long string of saliva dripping from his mouth, his mad eyes rimmed with white. He was panting, and his leaps were short of their mark, so he had to scramble back up the rocks, howling in powerless fury.

A moment later the dik-dik managed to slip away into a dense clump of thornbush. Gone, Morengáru thought, gloating a little, and it was only then that the obvious question occurred to him: Why hadn't the dik-dik run away sooner? It must have heard the troop coming, and all the time the baboons had been having their midday rest it had stayed there under the bushes. Why?

The moment Morengáru started moving, he caught Gray's eye. It was something he would never forget. His glance met the ape's, and with a breath-stopping shock he realized that here was one hunter looking at another. That look couldn't mean anything else. Gray might be a baboon, and he himself a human, but right then they were both first and foremost hunters. That was the only thing that mattered. That was why a single glance was all they needed to understand each other.

"Come and join me, but be careful and make a detour." That was the message, there could be no doubt about it.

From the corner of his eye, Morengáru could just see that the troop had given up their pursuit and were returning slowly, looking disappointed. In another moment they would have forgotten all about the dik-dik. Another moment, and no one would give it another thought, except the two hunters—one in the branches of the acacia and one in the knee-high grass.

They kept exchanging glances while Morengáru moved in a wide arc to get behind the bushes from which the dik-dik had sprung. Gray kept looking down and then back at him. His amber eyes were surprisingly light in his square doglike head. He raised his eyebrows repeatedly—something a baboon did only when excited—and his mane was bristling. And, strangely, he didn't make a sound. That proved once again how special this old baboon was. Baboons liked nothing better than being noisy. All day long you had to put up with screaming, growling, cackling, and squealing of all sorts, something Morengáru would never get used to.

Morengáru had reached the shrubs. He had no doubt that somewhere in there—pressed flat to the ground, trusting to its camouflage color—a dik-dik calf was hidden. That was why the dik-dik had not immediately fled. And when eventually it did, it was to divert attention from her young. The calf would stay motionless till the last possible moment, and take flight only when it was discovered.

Morengáru peered into the bushes. Plenty of dark spots amongst the lowest branches for a dik-dik calf to hide. But Gray knew where the animal was. Gray gave him directions with his eyes.

49

Morengáru could hardly believe he had actually hit the dik-dik calf—not even when he heard its backbone snap under the sharp blow of his club.

Gray let himself drop from the acacia, and Morengáru knew he had to be quick. Of course he was ready to share his prey with the big baboon, but he didn't want him to get away with the whole carcass. And he had neither a knife nor sharp fangs to tear open the dik-dik. He had to leave that job to Gray who, being a baboon, had never heard of sharing.

The calf was no larger than a rabbit. Just a tiny morsel. Gray effortlessly tore it in half and greedily appropriated the guts. He pressed the contents out between his fingers and ate with relish. Morengáru managed to grab the two hind legs. The meat was so tender he hardly had to chew it.

By now the others had noticed what was going on, and Gray's two allies came to join them. In no time, all that was left were a couple of bits of skin and the head. Morengáru broke open the skull with a rock and ate the soft brain. The rest he threw to Baldy, who sat begging excitedly nearby. Then he leaned back and shut his eyes. The energy drained out of him. Around him, the baboons squabbled over a leftover bone. Their mouths were covered in blood, and the sound of their gnawing teeth seemed deafening.

Morengáru had put his spear-club on the ground, and when he opened his eyes he saw Gray squatting next to it, examining the curious object intently. A bit later, with a glance at Morengáru as if asking permission, he picked it up. He had seen what Morengáru had done with it. Now he started swinging the club up and down awkwardly. It was making him excited.

Morengáru grinned. "Nice, eh?" he said softly. "You can learn a few things with that."

Gray dropped the stick again and squatted, looking at it for a long time. You'd swear he was thinking, trying to understand what he had seen. Morengáru couldn't help himself. He picked up the club and hurled it with all his might at the baobab. The wood hit the trunk with a bang. When he looked back at Gray, a bit triumphant despite himself, he saw to his surprise that his mane was raised. The animal stared at the club and then back at Morengáru.

"Good?" said Morengáru. He walked over to the baobab to retrieve his new weapon.

Shifty-eyes got there first. Morengáru had no idea where he had sprung from so suddenly. He picked up the club, jumped in the air, and raced off with it. Morengáru cursed himself. He should have been more careful with his new weapon. Shifty-eyes would carry the club around for a while, then lose interest and casually drop it somewhere, and Morengáru would never find it again.

Gray surprised him once more. With amazing speed for his age he stormed after Shifty-eyes, who wasn't ready for this at all. With an awesome display of fury the leader jumped right on top of the thief. Shifty-eyes yelled with shock and fear, dropped the club, and hastily limped away. In those few seconds, Gray had almost managed to twist off one of Shifty-eyes' legs. Now Gray sat staring at Morengáru's weapon again, as quietly as before.

Morengáru took his time, and when he reached him, Gray had picked up the club again. Of course, Morengáru should have known better, but he had not expected the big baboon to resist him. No matter how he threatened with raised eyebrows, gestures, and gaping mouth, Gray was not impressed and wouldn't return the club. Even loud gnashing of teeth had no effect. Gray smacked his lips a bit, as if to reassure him, but kept hold of the weapon. He wasn't really acting in a challenging way, but Morengáru couldn't allow his authority to be undermined like this. He saw the others watching him and knew he couldn't afford to lose face.

Morengáru calmed down. He turned away from Gray as if he had lost interest in the club, pretending that his attention had been drawn by something in the distance. Suddenly, he leaped up, shouting—not at Gray, but at some unseen danger. Simple as it was, the trick worked. Gray's mane instantly stood up, and he turned in the same direction as Morengáru.

The club, forgotten, slipped from his hand. For the sake of the performance, Morengáru walked a little way in the direction of the imagined danger, then pretended he was reassured and allowed himself to relax. Gray stayed next to him for a while, watchfully, looking at him steadily with his dark, questioning eyes.

Morengáru smiled to himself and went to pick up his club.

50

Gray knew exactly where certain fruits grew for miles around. And not just that—he also knew when they were ready to eat. How that could be was a puzzle to Morengáru. One day the old ape would resolutely lead the troop, crossing a whole, bare plain to arrive at a group of wild fig trees. And the fruit always turned out to be ripe on that day. How could Gray know things like that—and so much else besides? You'd almost think he carried some sort of calendar in that head of his. He was the memory for the whole troop. No wonder he was treated with respect; the others must have realized they needed his experience.

And as for tracking, Gray appeared to be at least as interested as Morengáru himself. He frowned shrewdly at the ratlike prints of the mongoose or at the fine, precise imprint left by a genet. And he knew which prints belonged to which animal, as Morengáru discovered to his amazement one day when they crossed the fresh track of a leopard. His reaction was only too clear: raised manes, growling, bared teeth. Gray must have encountered leopards before, that was clear.

He had another surprising habit, too. On some moonlit nights the baboons came down from their sleeping tree and held a procession—that's the only thing you could call it. Gray was always in front, followed by the other leaders, then the females with the young, and then the half-grown animals. They walked around the tree, sometimes including the baobab in their mysterious circle. Gray would always growl in a particular way, the others joining in at intervals. You'd swear it was some sort of ceremony, their growling a sort of chant.

"Hey, Gray, are you some kind of a *mundumugu?*"

Whenever Morengáru used his human voice, Gray would tilt his head back, a gesture that allowed him to look the other in the eyes. Normally, the protruding ridge of his eyebrows, which protected his eyes from the blinding sun on the plains, would get in the way.

If only he could reply. As time passed, Morengáru longed for conversation. He began to see his companions in a different light. Where at first he had been impressed with their "human" abilities, he now began to feel that something very important was lacking—even in the amber eyes of Gray.

155

It was impossible to have a conversation, to share thoughts; impossible to remind each other of the past or imagine the future together. For the baboons the only reality was the present. They were completely occupied with what was in front of them.

If I'm slowly turning into an ape, I'm still an ape who thinks about himself, Morengáru thought bitterly. With no one to talk to, and all these thoughts in my head, I must be going a bit mad. It's making my head heavy. What happens to thoughts that can't get out?

He couldn't help thinking about the bizarre life he now led, and how it had all come about. Usually, tired of worrying, he resigned himself to reality and tried not to brood. Besides, he had to keep up, to make sure everything edible wasn't snatched away from in front of his nose.

"You have to eat, for you show no signs of dying."

All the same, he sometimes got the overwhelming feeling all this wasn't real, that he was still dreaming feverishly in the baobab. Surely it couldn't be true that he was living here like an ape?

51

Baboons' lives were quite monotonous. They hated anything new and felt no need for variety. They trekked around in the same small circle, along the same well-trodden paths, and never ventured outside their own territory.

Birth, life, and death took place in a small area of the savanna, and the troop stayed mainly in a few defined places even within those limits. Everything baboons needed was to be found there: food, water, and a tree for sleeping.

Their routine was the same every day. Drowsily waking up at sunrise, eating for a while, moving along some way and then a dozy midday rest, the adults grooming each other or lazing in the shade while the tireless young continued to play around. Then back in marching order, searching for food, eating for a couple of hours, and returning to the sleeping tree in the evening, one by one climbing up to their own branch. Then everything became calm and silent up there. And so it went. . . .

This daily routine had a numbing effect on Morengáru. Each day was like every other, and time ceased to exist. He began to be irritated by all sorts of trivial things. The most wearing thing was that he always had to stay with the troop and take part in everything. You couldn't get away alone without some young males coming after you, curious to see what you were up to all by yourself. So they had first to be persuaded, with all the usual twisting and sniffing, that there was nothing worthwhile doing. Without that you just couldn't get rid of them.

And then there was their perpetual need to groom you. You had to allow it now and then to keep up your standing in the troop, but pretty quickly you got fed up with this plucking at hair and eyebrows. It took up a lot of time, and particularly at twilight, there was no escaping it.

Sometimes Morengáru would be struck by a burst of fury. The others seemed to sense this coming and made themselves scarce. He would hit the ground to left and right with his club and rip leaves and twigs from the bushes. When he was like this, the leaders avoided him, growling, and tried to call him to order in a submissive sort of way, but without

157

much conviction. It was as if they thought: Leave him to rage for a while, it'll pass.

And it did. His fury would abate, and he would sit down, calmly, a bit ashamed of himself. And then he would behave himself again, as if nothing had happened.

At other times he would suddenly get depressed. The others didn't notice this at all, except for Gray, perhaps. Gray sometimes came and sat down near him, looking at him quizzically with his yellow eyes. Once, Morengáru couldn't resist the temptation to pat him on his rough head. Gray reacted as if he had been reprimanded, and turned away. But soon he turned back and sniffed Morengáru's hand briefly. And after that, casually looking the other way, he shifted his tail toward Morengáru.

To his surprise, Morengáru was moved when he could feel Gray's tail curling around his ankles. Gray kept looking the other way, as if unaware of what his tail was doing. But after a while, he moved his heavy, rough body again and sat with his head turned to Morengáru, his snout close, with an intense look in his baboon eyes.

And then he made that one mysterious, throaty sound that Morengáru had never been able to understand. Gray said, "*Oohrrrng.*" And then once more, softly, "*Oohrrrng.*"

52

Morengáru had always been proud of his fast, instinctive reflexes, his "sixth sense," but some unexpected instincts surfaced in him now. He began to realize that over the centuries humans had lost many of these abilities because of the way they lived. He became aware, for instance, of the terror reaction.

You couldn't call it anything else, that one infinitesimal moment when you felt that something was wrong, that something was about to happen, without knowing what or why. You reacted instantly, the way you reacted to a sudden loud noise.

The baboons were completely familiar with this terror reaction. A group of baboons together on a branch might all look sleepy, but that was only the appearance. One of them was always alert. If that one spotted danger, he often didn't make a sound or even move. A slight tremor would go through him, which transmitted itself to all the others.

In the beginning, Morengáru had thought that all the baboons sat so close to each other to keep warm, for it could get bitterly cold at night on the plain. But he soon discovered otherwise. They stayed in bodily contact with each other even while asleep, so that the slightest shock was enough to bring the whole troop wide awake. It was like a wave of fright passing through them, and you could see even the ape right at the end of the line being affected.

Only the younger, playful animals weren't part of this, mainly because they liked to go on fooling about for a while at dusk. Like human children, they were fond of games, particularly turning somersaults and playing tag. And on their own sleeping branch they often tried to push each other off until only the strongest and most skillful remained. The adults would sit and watch them, chuckling sleepily.

No matter how rough baboons were with each other, they would never bother a pregnant female. A birth would happen in a secluded spot, some distance away from the sleeping tree. Morengáru had discovered that the sentries would position themselves so that they could keep an eye on the birthing place.

A newborn baboon attracted everyone's interest, and even the high-spirited young males were quiet when they eagerly came to have a look. Two or three of the leaders, who seemed to have proclaimed themselves uncles, screened mother and child from any overly intrusive curiosity.

Later the other females were allowed to touch the baby, but only after having begged at length. There was a lot of squabbling and pushing, until the novelty wore off.

A baby was carried until it could walk independently, at first clamped protectively against its mother's belly, later riding jauntily on her back. Later still, it would climb boldly on to the back of one of the "uncles." And if the troop was out on a raid, a little one would even climb from one back onto another. The more independent it became, the more it tried to get away from its mother's constant care. You could hear it protesting loudly if it was being cleaned and groomed too long for its liking. And if it tried to run away, the mother would casually hold onto its tail, often causing a real fit of temper.

Once a young one was too big to be suckled, it was in for a hard spell. The mother had to get her child used to solid food, and so she refused it more frequently when it demanded a drink. Then you could hear the young one howling with impotent fury, but strangely enough, even its "aunts" and "uncles" failed to listen. So it would soon seek comfort with its contemporaries. Before long, you could see it romping around with them all day, and the night would come when it no longer returned to the safety of its mother's arms.

53

One night, Morengáru heard one of the females scream so piteously that it sent a cold shiver down his spine. The scream turned into a long wail. Other baboons joined in.

Reluctantly he crawled out of his sleeping tree. Then, in the moonlight, he saw something he had never seen before. All the baboons were moving toward the sound. There was no screeching or barking, and their soft growling sounded ominous to Morengáru.

Even the sentries quietly left their posts and came down. They surrounded the wailing female, looking with outstretched necks, manes raised, and shaking with agitation. Morengáru was puzzled. He thought he had learned to recognize various dangers from the sounds the animals made, but this keening was new.

More baboons were wailing as the troop gathered, and when Morengáru approached, they didn't move, or even turn their heads. It was only now he recognized the female.

Where was her young?

Morengáru looked around. Had she dropped it in her sleep? Impossible. But then where was it? Why weren't the other apes looking for it? Did they know something he didn't know?

This noise was getting on his nerves. Even Gray had joined in. Morengáru felt excluded. If only someone could explain what was happening. Annoyed, he crawled back into his hollow tree, but he got no more sleep that night, for the crying noise started up again and again.

The sound was so ominous that he felt deeply worried for the first time in ages. Something dire must have happened, but what?

54

At first light Morengáru found his answer. He hadn't forgotten how to read tracks. A leopard had visited. A particularly cunning leopard who, silent as a shadow, had got close to the sleeping tree and snatched the baby.

It couldn't be helped. The leopard had always been the baboons' archenemy. Obviously the others agreed, for in the morning the whole troop got on with the daily routine as if nothing had happened. The leopard occupied Morengáru's thoughts for a while, but he forgot about the incident when he had to protect Baldy against Shifty-eyes.

The days flowed into each other again as if time didn't exist. For a few days there was heavy rain, which altered the routine a little. Often the apes would rather sit freezing under a mimosa tree than go out looking for food in the wet. But after the rain there was a time of plenty. Young shoots sprouted everywhere, and the plain, so barren before, was covered with small flowers.

In those peaceful days, there was only one incident. Shifty-eyes was suddenly attacked by the whole troop. Not that they seriously tried to hurt him, but he did get a good hiding. From then on he lagged behind a little, his ugly dog's face sulky. Morengáru gloated over him.

Morengáru didn't think of the leopard again until he was woken again by an agonizing cry. This time he knew immediately what was going on. His first thought was: What can I do about it?

Perhaps, as king of the baboons, he was expected to come rushing out—but it was already too late. What was the sense in sitting in a huddle all night, moaning? The leopard had obviously discovered an easy way of getting food. The sleeping apes were not prepared for such a stealthy night visitor. It might never occur to them to set sentries during the night. Was he supposed to go and do that all by himself?

And what then? The baboons at least had their fearsome fangs. If it came to a fight, they were at least as fast as a leopard. But he . . .

Was he supposed to tackle a leopard with a stick?

55

The leopard's third victim was Baldy.

This time it wasn't the wailing of a grieving mother that woke Morengáru, but the scream of an ape in mortal terror. The shrieks pierced the silence of the night, and the next moment growling and barking sounded all around. The baboons dropped out of the tree, fearless and ready for a fight.

What you couldn't hear was the leopard. He managed to vanish as silently as he had come, carrying the baboon in his mouth.

It troubled Morengáru. He noticed that Gray wasn't his usual self, either. The old ape kept searching as the troop moved over the plain. It took days before he was back to normal. And Morengáru kept thinking about Baldy. Time and again, he remembered how that brazen ape would get up to all sorts of tricks, when he knew his back was covered. Unable to put these images out of his mind, Morengáru became irritable.

But there was something more: Baldy wasn't a defenseless

young animal. Obviously, this leopard wasn't afraid of grabbing a half-grown male. Baldy must have fought back. Yet the great cat had dragged him away, despite the whole troop immediately swinging into action. It must be a big, powerful leopard.

The terror reaction, which would alert the whole troop, didn't work for the young on their own branch, but neither did it work for that one, superior 'baboon' who was the lone inhabitant of the baobab. And how much trouble would this cunning leopard have with the few branches that were supposed to protect Morengáru against intruders?

Perhaps it was time to leave.

But how could he live without the troop? Who would protect a cripple from the predators of the plain? And where could he go?

Morengáru rolled himself up small in the hollow trunk of the baobab, muttering a half-forgotten spell.

Better stay. Perhaps the leopard wouldn't come back at all, and if he did it would be too much of a coincidence if he picked Morengáru.

Plenty of young or half-grown males, bald or otherwise. The troop had managed for centuries without human help. They didn't need him. He was their king only in name. Ridiculous to think that obliged him to act. What could he do?

Morengáru curled up even tighter in the baobab. But it no longer made him feel secure. He felt the sharp point of his spear-club with his fingers.

A worthless weapon.

What else could he do but wait?

56

When the leopard returned again, and the scream of a young ape broke the night, Morengáru sprang up, full of his old hunting passion. But as he clambered laboriously out of the baobab, he could feel the excitement rapidly fade. The passion might still be there, but he no longer had the strength or the skill to respond. Hanging half out of the hole in the baobab, he stared into the night, cursing his powerlessness.

In the white moonlight, the first thing he saw was the leopard. For a single moment he couldn't recognize that black shadow slipping away under the mimosa. He had been prepared to see a spotted hide, but then he understood. A black leopard.

Any leopard was a formidable opponent, but there was something especially fearsome about a black one. In the *mundumugus'* gruesome leopard stories, black leopards played a large, often shocking role. Even if he were the Morengáru of old, he would have thought twice before daring to tangle with one of those uncanny animals.

The leopard bit through the young baboon's throat. All resistance and crying stopped. But before the beast could get away with its prey, the rough shape of Gray, roaring fearsomely, came hurtling down from the branches of the mimosa.

The old ape should have known better. Perhaps he did. Surrounded by adult males, a leopard would probably go under. But Gray by himself, with his worn fangs . . . he didn't have a chance. Even so, he hurled himself at the great cat, who let go of his prey, turned with lightning speed, and rolled on his back. He lashed out just once with the terrible claws on his hind legs. . . .

Morengáru screamed. He knew what had happened even before he could see it. He knew the effect of those fearful claws. Gray was flung back, his belly ripped open, and his roar changed to a long shriek of pain. He doubled up and rolled over and over. Morengáru stared. He wasn't aware that he was screaming as loudly and as long as Gray. And when the screaming stopped, Morengáru collapsed onto the ground as if there was no life left in his body.

57

Before dawn, a strange ceremony took place. At first Morengáru didn't understand its meaning. He sat apart from the others, crushed, devastated, staring at Gray's body. He knew what would happen later. He had observed before what the baboons did with a body when one of them died. They usually dragged it away and threw it into a ravine nearby, where the dense undergrowth would hide the carcass from view. A kind of burial, as if they wanted to banish death from their midst.

But this time was different. This time all the animals in the troop, young and old, formed a kind of procession. It reminded him of the mysterious ceremonies they used to hold on moonlit nights, led by Gray himself. This time, the old ape was last in the line, the others dragging him along by his legs. The half-grown animals led, followed by the females and the young, and finally the leaders with their dead burden.

First they walked around their sleeping tree, then they

included the baobab in their ceremonial circle. They all growled in a particular way, like a kind of chanting, and to his surprise, Morengáru joined in. He too plodded along in line; he too growled, and as befitted a funeral, his heart was heavy with grief.

Having completed the circle round the baobab, the leaders dragged the lifeless body over the rough grass, a quarter of a mile away to the "burial ground."

There went Gray. His great, rough, gray body moved one last time. He rolled down the slope, hurtling head over heels and as if he were hunting one more time, he shot into the dense tangle of scrub.

Morengáru sat at the top of the ravine long after the others had returned to their sleeping tree. Slowly it dawned on him what Gray's death would mean. Very soon, the power struggle between the old ape's two allies would flare up. Who emerged victorious was irrelevant; the winner's next step would be to challenge Morengáru and dispute his "kingship." Either way, it seemed likely that his time with the baboon troop was coming to an end.

What now?

The simplest solution would be to let himself roll down the slope after Gray. Somewhere down there, in the scrub, the grave diggers would be avidly waiting for him, too.

"Are you there, *fisi*, my friend?"

He had felt this urge a few times lately. The temptation to give in was greater than ever. But something stopped him. There was something to be done first. He remembered Baldy's *tsjilp-tsjilp-tsjilp*. Baldy, who had been the first to come and look at him with concern in the baobab. Dead. He remembered Gray's mysterious *oohrrrng* and his dark, questioning look. Dead.

Someone would have to pay for their deaths. Someone was going to regret he had attacked those two. From now on, Morengáru the hunter would be on the leopard's trail.

The leopard had to die.

Without emotion, Morengáru remembered the crying of the grieving females. That was simply nature's way. And stupid Baldy had really asked for it. But every time he thought of Gray, he felt a stab of guilt. Gray had done what the king of the baboons should have done.

Gray must be avenged.

PART 6

at the end of the gorge

58

It rained continuously. The baboons, soaked and numb with cold, lost interest in everything. They huddled together, their backs turned against the gusting rain, water trickling from their wet fur.

Often, Morengáru saw his face reflected in the many puddles all around. He stared hollow-eyed, amazed at the pent-up fury in the eyes of the wrinkled death's-head glaring back at him.

What had got into him? The leopard's tracks had long since been washed away by the rain.

"But he'll come back. He'll come back, you can be sure of it."

And then? What then? What could a cripple like him do against a leopard?

"If he comes back, he'll grab another young. And you can't stop him."

Arr-ah! Arr-ah!

He wasn't even any use as a sentry, locked up in the dark center of the baobab. And yet somehow the black leopard's raids had to be stopped.

But how?

He'd worry about that later. First the leopard had to return. He had to come back to do what he had to do. And then leave behind what he had to leave behind. His tracks.

"And then, Morengáru, what then?"

No *moran* spear, no poison arrows, not even a *parang*.

"Do you tackle leopards with your bare hands these days?" The hollow face in the puddle of water smirked bitterly. "Think, Morengáru, think carefully. There must be a way. You can't throw a spear or shoot an arrow, none of those things—but you can track and you can think."

More rain washed over his face. More rain paralyzed the baboon troop. More rain brought cold and hunger, and gradually the deprivation brought him to a state of exhaustion. And exhaustion brought visions—dream images he lived through, half waking, half asleep.

Morengáru saw fields of long, spiky green blades, the points black and sharp. He knew what it was: a tough species of grass that grew in clumps on the savanna. In times of drought, you could press moisture from those fleshy stalks. But why was he thinking of that grass now, in the wet season?

It took two days of drowsing and dreaming under the leaky roof of the baobab for the significance of that recurring vision to penetrate his mind. And then suddenly he knew, without logical thought. Just as mysteriously as the vision had come to him, the solution, too, appeared before his eyes.

Of course! You picked one of those fleshy stalks and beat it on a stone until all the soft pulp was crushed and could be scraped off. And then what was left? A long, tough, flexible rib.

And you could twist a handful of those tough ribs into a solid cord, and also . . . a net.

Not a net to carry fruits. Not a net for fishing. A big, strong net to catch the leopard.

59

As long as the rain continued, the baboons showed no interest in what Morengáru was up to. For days on end he was busy picking and treating the stiff blades, as tall as a man. Then he twisted the ribs into strong strands, using his teeth when he couldn't manage with his one good hand. But eventually the change in his behavior made the leaders curious. They must have thought that the baboon king was playing.

They couldn't accept that. It lowered their respect for him. It was one thing for young males to be a bit playful at times, but an adult baboon should know what was expected: a serious and dignified attitude. This fiddling with blades of grass was absolutely pointless. What was going on?

Shifty-eyes was the first to try and take away Morengáru's "toys." Morengáru hadn't seen him coming and instinctively pulled his lips back and bared his teeth. Shifty-eyes hurriedly withdrew. Morengáru carried on working. He could think of nothing except his net. He stumbled for miles over the sodden plain looking for more clumps of swordgrass. The baboons, cold and miserable under their sleeping tree, watched him with blank eyes. Only curious Shifty-eyes followed him at times.

The net took weeks. Patiently, he kept at it. Meanwhile, there were some dry spells. And with the sun, warmth returned. And with warmth, the baboons revived. Very soon, the struggle for leadership flared between Gray's two former allies. At first there was just a lot of hissing, screaming, and outward show of strength. But it was obvious that a violent clash couldn't be far away.

It may have been his imagination, but it seemed to

Morengáru that Shifty-eyes was trying to inflame the situation. More and more, the hypocrite behaved like a troublemaker. And he drew the others' attention to Morengáru's activities, as if to say: Just look at what our king is doing! Playing with grass!

Gradually, Morengáru became blind to everything except his net. No less than three times, one of the adult baboons tried to snatch that precious weapon away from him. Instantly, Morengáru lashed out with his club and hit the angry ape over the head. He didn't even notice the fangs he had always feared. The terrible claws now left him indifferent. His good arm handled the club as if it were part of him. *Whack!*—and the most aggressive of the males slunk off with his tail between his legs. *Bang!*—and one of the leaders hurried away. Morengáru wasn't even aware of it, but at last he really was the leader, the boss, the one with clout—in short, the king of the baboons.

And the work progressed. The twisted grass stalks grew into a large net, tough, indestructible, able to withstand the blind strength of a captured beast of prey—the rage of a trapped leopard.

60

Then Morengáru worked out where he was going to find the leopard. The solution came to him in exactly the same way as the idea for the net.

He started off by looking for tracks, but the constant showers washed away every trace. For too many hours, Morengáru squatted by the very last of the last signs, guessing where the trail might lead next. Each time he returned to the baobab, disappointed and defeated. It was hopeless. Even the best tracker would fail here. A couple of hours of sun was simply not enough. After one or two miles of a painstaking search, another downpour washed away any signs. Dejected, he squatted under the baobab, his net rolled up between his knees. The apes sat around him in groups, gaping curiously. He gnashed his teeth.

The final cloudburst was the heaviest they'd had for a long time. The rain came down so hard it seemed to wash every thought out of his head, but deep inside him an image appeared. A path. The way the leopard must have gone.

Who needed tracks? He could laugh at the rain. No one could confuse him, nothing could lead him astray. He *knew* the way. He *was* the leopard. The rain had brought the dream, and the dream pointed the way.

He set out.

He was so absorbed in his plan, so concentrated on the waiting task, that at first he forgot about his "subjects." Only when he discovered they were no longer following did he realize he would need their help. Catching the leopard was his task, but killing it he would have to leave to them. That's what was decided, somewhere deep inside him, somewhere in the dream. But the baboons had different ideas. They had not been part of his scheme, and they knew nothing of his dream. If only he could explain it to them. If only he could say, "Follow me, and we'll catch the black leopard, the killer of our children, the murderer of Baldy and Gray. Follow me, and we'll trap him and kill him like vermin. Follow me, and he won't stand a chance. I, your leader, will go before you. I, your tracker, will know where to find him."

The baboons yawned. They shivered and raised their

eyebrows. No matter whether he spoke human language or made baboon sounds, they were deaf to him. They didn't want to leave the shelter of the mimosa tree. They feared the rain-drenched openness of the plain. They couldn't see what they had to seek there. They didn't understand him.

Many times Morengáru took off, trying to lure his troop with every trick he had learned. He lifted stones from under which any snails or ants had long since gone. He plucked branches long since eaten bare. He feigned excitement at finding nothing—all in vain. Occasionally he managed to attract a few of the young males, but most of the troop showed no interest whatsoever. He went back to the baobab, defeated.

One morning he woke with a very strong feeling that he had lost something. He saw Shifty-eyes running away, carrying something in his hands. His precious net! The next moment, he had overtaken Shifty-eyes. Later, he could remember the crunching blow of his club and the snarl as Shifty-eyes tried to bite him, missing his face by a fraction. He even remembered the exact moment his club shut Shifty-eyes' left eye permanently—but what he could not remember was the sprint that enabled him to catch Shifty-eyes.

How had he done it? How had he managed, with his crippled leg, to get up such speed? He sat grinning and puzzling about that, with his net in his hands, while Shifty-eyes slunk away, whining. "Oh, Morengáru, was that you running? Had you forgotten you were half paralyzed?"

Why was he feeling so satisfied, just because he had his net back? With diabolical pleasure he watched Shifty-eyes, who had gone off to complain to his followers, a group of young males who had been trying vainly to join the ranks of the leaders. Stupid ape, he thought, next time I'll shut your other eye for you. And don't any of you dare come anywhere near my net, you pack of idiots! This net is going to save you. But how do I get that into your skulls? You're too thick-headed to understand what I'm doing, you mob of half-wit apes!

61

It took him ages to gather enough seeds, nuts, and fruits to feed the whole troop for two days. All that time, he felt nothing but fury and contempt. He went about cursing and swearing loudly, getting drenched by occasional showers.

Of course the baboons discovered his store, and of course they tried to get it away from him, but his club reached everywhere at once, and he didn't hesitate to use his teeth when necessary. To his own amazement, when Shifty-eyes ventured too close, he found himself at his throat, biting like a real baboon. In short, as he told himself with grim satisfaction, he behaved like a real baboon king.

The day came when there wasn't a cloud from horizon to horizon, and the sunlight slanted over the plain.

Now! thought Morengáru. Now! And he set off.

It was as if the troop could sense that this time he wouldn't retrace his steps. A few baboons followed him immediately, and the others joined them after only a little hesitation. It was different from the other times. Perhaps Morengáru radiated certainty, for he was determined he would carry on, no matter what. He would find the leopard.

Around midday he scattered handfuls of food between the shrubs and the freshly sprouting grass. The baboons closest to him enjoyed this sudden abundance, and their excitement and lip-smacking brought the others running. So Morengáru got the whole troop together again.

After giving his subjects time to eat, he went on, leaning on his club, the net over his shoulder. The baboons followed.

The path he had seen in his dream led to a gorge. He was not surprised. Of course it had to be a gorge that would lead him to the leopard. By now, he considered the leopard his oldest enemy. And the most recent. The eternal enemy. The gorge that led to the leopard was new to him, yet familiar— no different from the gorge that had led him from the Loita hills to a new and uncertain existence. But this gorge turned out to be the worst of them all. It was deep, filled with mist, dark. When it rained in this gorge, the thunder rolled back and forth between the walls, and lightning flashed everywhere.

The baboons had no business here. They didn't want to be here. The gorge was gloomy, drafty, lifeless; nothing but bare walls and black granite. It was so dark and chill that they felt ill at ease right from the start. The sound of falling water came at them from all sides, and the wind howled through cracks in the rocks.

Morengáru was convinced he was heading the right way. He no longer even looked for tracks. He knew for sure where the gorge would take him, as if he had been that way before.

The baboons only knew that the gorge was full of gray mist and that water dripped everywhere, even when it wasn't raining. The sun couldn't penetrate that mist, and nothing would dry in that dank air. As soon as Morengáru stopped to rest, they sat shivering and smirking—a peevish, reluctant troop, led by the hand that scattered food in their path. Dumb hulks whom he needed, and gradually came to hate.

"Morons. Why don't you just follow me? I'll lead you to the leopard. I'll capture him for you in this net so you can tear him apart like a dik-dik calf. Do I have to lure you along with a few miserable nuts and seeds?"

If only Gray were still here. Several times Morengáru came across the leopard's tracks without even looking for them, but the baboons showed no sign of recognition. If the leopard's scent was in the air at all, it was so indistinct Morengáru couldn't smell it. The stench and the noise of the troop must be driving the beast farther and farther ahead. But somewhere at the end of the gorge he must have a lair, an inaccessible shelter where he would take cover.

The mist became thicker and turned into darkness as evening fell. They found a cave, as sinister as the gorge itself, where the sharp scent of bats overpowered even the smell of the baboons. There was something frightening about that scent, and the bats unsettled the baboons. Every now and then you could hear the flapping of their wings in the dark, or a piercing squeak that hurt your ears. The freezing baboons huddled close together, miserable and lost. They couldn't understand what they were doing here. If they hadn't been so afraid of the dark, they would have rushed back to the plain. All night Morengáru listened to their growling and gnashing.

The next morning he scattered the rest of the food on the path that led farther upward. There wasn't much left. He ate nothing himself. He was shivering, and cursed the baboons who followed him more and more unwillingly. He was close to giving up. Cursing and yelling, he went on ahead of the troop, climbing awkwardly with his lame leg.

But he forgot his misery the instant the gorge ended in a small cave. Like all holes and cracks in a rock face, the cave should have been covered in cobwebs, but there was no sign of them here. He tried to see inside, but little light penetrated the gloom. Just a glimpse of sky showed through a hole in the roof at the back.

Morengáru knew enough. He was certain this was the leopard's hiding place. The baboons must have worked it out, too, for their attitude suddenly changed. They forgot the cold and the damp and sat gaping and threatening with bristling manes. No doubt they could smell something he couldn't. None of them made a move to go in. The leopard had to be in there. One of the leaders started up a loud, shrill *waaf*, and the whole troop became terribly excited.

Finally, they knew why they were here. The situation was clear. All he had to do now was make sure the black leopard came out.

He unrolled his net and fixed it to projections in the rockface. That took a lot of patience and agility. More than once, the cheekiest of the males tried to snatch the net away. Morengáru, absorbed in what he was doing, lashed out blindly with his club. He wielded it in such a domineering way that he convinced the troop of his unchallengeable leadership. It took him till midday to fix the net securely. Billowing gently in the wind, it now completely blocked the entrance to the cave.

The next part was the hardest. It would be really difficult for him to climb the steep rock, and he also had to stop the troop following him. Gingerly, he started clambering up, inching along ledges. Every time a baboon started to follow him, he kicked it mercilessly in the head. They *had* to stay down. They had to be ready to catch the leopard in that one moment when it would get tangled in the net. What would happen after that, he could safely leave to them.

The climb exhausted him. Suspended between heaven and earth, his cheek pressed against the rock, he despaired of the whole scheme. In the end, the reason he kept climbing up was simple: Getting down in one piece was out of the question. By then, no baboons were following him. They were staring upward with glittering teeth, shrieking and tense with excitement, as if they understood the purpose of it all. Morengáru reached the top at last. He sat down, trembling with fatigue. Sweat dripped into his eyes. But he allowed himself no rest. He crawled over to the hole that let light into the cave. A few small stones rattled down, but he didn't think the leopard could suspect what was going on above him. The threatening racket of the baboons must surely have distracted him.

The rest was simple. He no longer felt his old hunter's passion. It was a job to be done, that was all. The black leopard had claimed too many victims, and now it was his turn. Morengáru felt no satisfaction. Just indifference.

The opening was about two steps wide. Morengáru could see nothing below it. Not that he had expected to. A black leopard, flattening itself in the semidarkness! He searched for a large stone and crawled back to the opening, rolling it along because he couldn't carry it with his one hand. Out of the corner of his eye he could see the troop in the gorge, squatting in fighting order: males at the front, females and young at a safe distance. A half smile came over his face.

Then he dropped the stone through the opening.

62

Morengáru heard the stone hit the bottom of the cave. The sound echoed against the rock walls like thunder. Now slipping and sliding, now falling, crashing, and banging, it created a din like an avalanche. With the desired result. A furious, hissing screech rose from the darkness. Morengáru heard a deafening uproar from the baboons. With a little effort, he could have looked at what was going on at the entrance to the cave. He could have seen the leopard storm out and be hopelessly entangled in the treacherous net. The baboons would be savaging him from all sides. Their yells of victory told him enough. The leopard didn't have a chance.

But Morengáru didn't bother to crawl back. He had no need to see. Instead, he turned around and scrambled up the final stretch. Soon his head cleared the top of the gorge, and he looked out over an immense plain.

He stood up. For the first time in ages, he stretched out his deformed body. The brisk wind coming off the plain blew into his face, and he could no longer hear what was going on below. Eyes narrowed, he gazed over the sun-drenched hills. The grass, with its tall white plumes, undulated in the breeze. Everything looked green and fresh after all the rain. Far in the distance a gigantic rainbow stretched over two hilltops. And yet this was the same barren country he had trekked through, following One-horn's tracks. A herd of zebras grazed in the distance, and a pair of elands galloped close by, their brown bodies gleaming like velvet in the sunlight. As far as his eyes could see, the plain stretched out, bathed in that gentle glow.

Morengáru paused. It was as if he could see beyond the last line of hills, beyond the horizon and the high plateau, to where human habitation began. It was as if he could see gardens and round huts and grazing cattle and small boys guarding goats. It was as if he could see old men in a meeting, mumbling as always with slow, dignified gestures . . . and even the spear-carriers on the hilltops, shouting things at each other, laughing.

Leaning on his club, Morengáru started to walk. He dragged his lame leg along patiently. It would be a slow journey, but he had plenty of time. He had learned how to live off the land, and as long as he was going in the right direction, it was all fine by him. After a while, he started singing.

> Are you there? Show me where!
> I'm sick of standing here!
> This is no game!
> Morengáru is my name!